"I was waiting for you to come out
so that I cou   "
She lower
provoca
"I hop

He tried to avert his gaze, but she made it extremely difficult. She picked up her clothes from a nearby chair and catwalked toward him.

"Feeling better?" she asked. Her eyes moved slowly over him, then returned to his face.

He could feel the heat radiating off her. "Yeah. Much."

She reached out to touch his bare shoulder. He turned his head in her direction and before he could react she kissed him, her full chest flush against his arm. Her soft moan was like a song in his ears. She pressed her body against his and he felt the quick tightening in his groin. Her arm snaked around his neck and with her free hand she tugged at the towel wrapped around his waist.

"Touch me," she whispered against his lips.

Books by Donna Hill

Kimani Romance

Love Becomes Her
If I Were Your Woman
After Dark
Sex and Lies
Seduction and Lies
Temptation and Lies
Longing and Lies
Private Lessons
Spend My Life with You
Secret Attraction

DONNA HILL

began writing novels in 1990. Since that time she has had more than forty titles published, including full-length novels and novellas. Two of her novels and one novella were adapted for television. She has won numerous awards for her body of work. She is also the editor of five novels, two of which were nominated for awards. She easily moves from romance to erotica, horror, comedy and women's fiction. She was the first recipient of the *RT Book Reviews* Trailblazer Award, won an *RT Book Reviews* Career Achievement Award and currently teaches writing at the Frederick Douglass Creative Arts Center.

Donna lives in Brooklyn with her family. Visit her website at www.donnahill.com.

SECRET
Attraction
DONNA HILL

KIMANI™
ROMANCE

KIMANI PRESS™

Recycling programs
for this product may
not exist in your area.

ISBN-13: 978-0-373-86208-5

SECRET ATTRACTION

www.kimanipress.com

Printed in U.S.A.

Dear Reader,

It is a blessing in life when you get to do what you love. Trust me, I am blessed! I have been given the opportunity to bring stories, issues and people to life that hopefully make you laugh, cry, shout, think, hug someone and seek out your significant other! And nothing tops creating a group of characters that you cannot wait to share with readers. That's what happened with the Lawsons of Louisiana.

Can you believe that in the twenty years of my writing career this is the first time I've actually developed a family? The first book, *Spend My Life with You*, introduced the Lawson clan and showcased the eldest daughter, Lee Ann. Now you will meet Desiree Lawson, one of the Lawson twins. Her twin sister, Dominique, has gotten Desiree into a hot mess, to say the least, and it just may cost her the one man she cares about—übersexy restaurateur Spence Hampton. Against a backdrop of politics, fast cars, sexy men, ex-girlfriends and dangerous suitors, *Secret Attraction* has something for everyone.

And, yes, the dashing, sexy bachelor brother Rafe Lawson is still hot and single. Rafe was introduced in *Heart's Reward*. So expect to hear his story soon!

I do hope you enjoy *Secret Attraction*. I love to hear from readers and I welcome your comments about the Lawsons of Louisiana. Who do you want to see featured next? Who is your favorite character? Let me know at dhassistant@gmail.com.

Until next time,

Donna

Chapter 1

The near-deafening roar of the red Ferrari's engine vaulted through her veins. Her limbs vibrated as the low-riding race car hurtled forward. Concentration and survivor's instinct took over as images left, right and center flew by too quickly for recognition. The speedometer teetered at 159 mph. *Oh, God.* The car held the ground on two wheels, barely missing the guardrail as it made the long turn and pointed straight ahead.

A plume of smoke burst on her right as motion met the inanimate concrete wall. *Almost there.* Her heart thundered in her ears. *Almost.* Red and white flashed in front of her. One hundred…ninety…seventy-five…fifty…thirty…twenty…

Within seconds she was surrounded. The door was yanked open and the smell of burnt rubber, exhaust fumes and gasoline swirled in the air.

She pulled off her helmet and a head full of wild spiral curls sprung out around her face like a dark auburn halo. Her five-foot-five inch frame was dwarfed by the towering, bulky pit crew. The throb of the engine still pumped through her veins. She stood on wobbly legs.

"Great job, D.J.," Mike, the pit boss, said, clapping her on the shoulders. "Took that turn like a pro. See you in two weeks?"

"As always," she said, pride and adrenaline lifting the corners of her full mouth. She made her way off the track, toward the locker room, while the team pushed the car away.

The locker room was no more than a testosterone-drenched boys' clubhouse, complete with backslapping, ribald jokes, cussing, beer guzzling and plenty of naked behinds. They'd grudgingly made room for her when she started racing about two years earlier, and once they witnessed her skill behind the wheel and her resolve to be respected in the locker room, she became one of the boys. Although there wasn't a man among them that wouldn't give his left nut for five minutes of her time off of the track.

To them she was just D.J., the pint-size race car dynamo that could beat some of the best of them on a bad day. Back home in Baton Rouge, she was Desiree Janel Lawson, twin sister to Dominique, younger sister to Rafe and Lee Ann, older sister to Justin and daughter of Senator Branford Lawson. In the cacophony of those larger-than-life personalities in the Lawson home, Desiree felt lost, a shadow. But here on the track she had found her footing, which wasn't one of a political celebrity, "the daughter of," "the twin sister to"—here she was a person with her own identity.

Weekend racing had become her secret passion over the years. She had always had a love for fast cars and would spend hours as a teenager watching the Indy 500 or the NASCAR races on television. She'd confessed to her twin sister, Dominique, that one day she would get behind the wheel of one of those babies, which Dominique had summarily dismissed as being ridiculous, dangerous and out of the question. What man in his right mind would want a woman who always smelled of fumes and gasoline? Not to mention that their father would be apoplectic and the press would have a field day.

So Desiree kept her dream to herself and began taking lessons in New Orleans, away from prying eyes. She could never come out publicly, she mused as she stripped out of her gear and got into the shower, but she could still enjoy her passion. The idea that it was her very own secret made what she did, twice a month, that much more exciting. The only one who knew about her "getaway Saturdays" was her best friend, Patrice Lamont, who was waiting in the lounge.

"You do realize I now have a heart condition because of you," Patrice said as the two walked through the building and out into the parking lot.

Desiree laughed. "I'm sure you'll be fine after lunch."

"Humph. So you say."

They'd driven down in Desiree's very conservative

black Volvo, a far cry from the lightning-fast Ferrari. Desiree's door locks chirped and they got in. She pushed the key into the ignition. "Where do you want to go for lunch?"

"How about Emeril's place in the Warehouse District?"

"Sure. We haven't been there in a while."

Desiree zipped the car out of the space.

"And, uh, try to keep the speed under seventy."

"Maybe."

Patrice sat back and held on—just in case.

Of course they arrived at Emeril's New Orleans in record time. Patrice barely had enough time to get her story out about the latest scandal on Capitol Hill in D.C. before they were being escorted to their table.

"This is not a good time to be under an ethics investigation in the middle of an election year," Patrice was saying as they sat down.

"No time is ever good. My biggest issue is that the Democratic Party, whenever they come into full power, winds up getting beat up on every issue by the Republicans. And instead of taking a stand, they collapse. They need to learn to fight below the belt, too." Desiree fanned open her menu.

Patrice shook her head. "I have to agree. We need some backbone."

"My two favorite guests."

Desiree and Patrice looked up into the ruggedly handsome face of Paul, the general manager.

He leaned down and kissed each of their cheeks. "How are you ladies today? It's been a while."

"Just fine, Paul," Desiree said. "I've been salivating thinking about the andouille and chicken jambalaya."

"I will oversee it myself." He turned his Mediterranean blue eyes on Patrice. "And what about you, Ms. Patrice?"

"I think I'll have the Creole fried chicken."

"Excellent choice. But, of course, whatever you choose at Emeril's is excellent. I'll put your orders in myself and send your waiter to get your drinks. Enjoy your meal."

"Hmm, if he wasn't gay, I would eat him up," Patrice said under her breath as she watched him walk away.

Desiree snickered. "I know you would. But what else is new?"

"Oh, don't go hating. Just because I have a lusty appetite for men…" She took a sip of her water, then took a lemon wedge from the china bowl on the table and squeezed it into the water.

Desiree looked at her from beneath her lashes and bit back a smile. *Lusty* was putting it mildly. Patrice had more men and more dates than she could keep up with. What she needed was a personal assistant to help her keep it all straight. There were times, though, that she envied Patrice and her cavalier attitude about men and sex, and her sister Dominique, as well. Certainly, she'd dated off and on, nothing really serious. Most of the men she met really wanted to get close to her sister Dominique or sought entrée into the political life dominated by her powerful father. So she tended to keep her love life, such as it was, to a minimum. But if she was truly honest with herself, the real reason was her attraction from afar to Spence Hampton. She'd spent too many nights wishing that it was her in the passenger seat of his car or that she was the recipient of his dimpled smile and hungry stares. They'd known each other since their late teens, when Dominique brought him to the house for one of the family's massive Independence Day barbecues. She thought her heart would stop and she had to concentrate on not staring at him. But Spence was her sister's friend, always had been, and that was a line that she didn't cross.

"You haven't heard a word I've said. What are you thinking about?"

Desiree blinked. How long had she been daydreaming? She gave a light toss of her head. "Sorry. Just the race." She focused on Patrice. "So…what were you saying?"

Patrice pursed her lips, feigning annoyance. "I was telling you we should double-date next weekend."

"Why?"

"Because you need to get out and I want to make sure that you do. Jay has a really cute friend."

Desiree propped her elbow on the table and rested her head in her palm. "And who is Jay, may I ask?"

Patrice frowned. "Didn't I tell you about Jay?"

"Uh, no."

"Oh." She waved her hand dismissively. "I met him at the Laundromat."

"What? Why were you in the Laundromat? You have a washer and dryer in your town house."

"And your point is?" Patrice picked up her glass of lemon-flavored water. "You can always tell who a man lives with by his laundry."

"Oh, right. What was I thinking." She shook her head as the waiter approached and placed their entrées in front of them.

"Can I get you ladies anything else?"

Patrice glanced up and ran her cinnamon-tinted eyes up and down his lean body, zeroed in on his name tag, then back up to his face. She ran the tip of her tongue across her bottom lip. "What would you suggest, Felix?" she asked, clearly not interested in anything on the menu.

Desiree had a mind to kick her under the table but watching Patrice in action was always fascinating.

A slow, lazy smile eased across his wide mouth. His lids lowered just a fraction over his dark eyes. "I'm sure I can find something that would interest you. A light wine or something a little stronger? And, of course, there is dessert," he added with only the slightest hint of his South American accent.

Patrice drew in a breath. "Yes, I think I'd be interested in dessert."

He turned to Desiree. "And you, ma'am?"

"I'm fine, thank you."

He gave a short nod to both women. "I'll bring the dessert menu."

Patrice returned her attention to her meal.

"How do you do that?"

Patrice glanced across the table. "Do what?"

"That! That thing you do with every man you meet."

Patrice frowned slightly. "You mean, let them know that they are totally male and I notice it?"

"Is that what you call it?" Desiree took a forkful of food.

Patrice shrugged her right shoulder. "I like men. Plain and simple. All kinds of men. Testing my attraction to them is exciting. It doesn't mean anything. It's just harmless flirting. You should try it. Let yourself go. It's very liberating."

Desiree swallowed slowly. "I don't want to flirt and tease and play games." She put down her fork. "I want something real and someone who is real with me. Is that so wrong?"

"Desi, you're much too serious. I have to tell you, if I wasn't your best friend and didn't know that you were this crazy, secret race car driver, I would think that you were really an uptight, reserved, conservative chick. But I know that you're not, sweetie. The thing is, it doesn't matter what I think. You have to be who you are." She raised her glass to her lips. "But you could always put a little more dip in those hips," she added with a wink and a smile.

Desiree thought about their conversation, one that they'd had on several occasions in the past, as she prepared for work at the city council. She'd always tossed off Patrice's commentaries about her lack of sustained or even intermittent relationships as Patrice's way of validating her own lifestyle. But the more she considered it, the more she had to admit that Patrice was probably more right than wrong. Although she'd never told anyone about her thing for Spence, not even Patrice, maybe it was long past time to forget him once and for all. So that she could actually find someone that could light that same spark in her the way Spence did whenever she saw him.

Maybe.

Chapter 2

"Got a delivery, boss," Jacques, the day manager, said, poking his head into the busy kitchen. All hands were busy preparing for the weekend rush.

Spence glanced over his left shoulder, not missing a beat while whisking his famed cream sauce to simply smooth perfection. "Have Michelle take a look. It should be the new glassware that I ordered."

"Will do." The door swung closed behind him.

Spence dipped a spoon into the sauce and took a small taste. His dark chocolate eyes momentarily closed in instant euphoria. "Peter," he called out with a lift of his cleft chin, peering across the rows of stainless-steel preparation tables, simmering pots and sizzling skillets. "Take over from here." He wiped his hands on his pristine white apron and began his preinspection of the menu.

As owner and executive chef of Bottoms Up, one of Baton Rouge's swankiest supper clubs, he was ultimately responsible for each and every thing that happened in his establishment, from the decor to the dessert. His goal was to make each experience for his guests an unforgettable one. Bottoms Up, since its opening five years earlier, had consistently been listed as a must-see destination in restaurant and entertainment magazines. For weekend seating, reservations often had to be made weeks in advance, and when major performers appeared, which was often, the club was packed from front to back.

Spence's skills in the kitchen were so renowned that he had been offered his own cooking show on more than one occasion and had done a stint on *Beyond Top Chefs* as one of the celebrated judges.

Much of his notoriety he could attribute to his long-time relationship with Dominique Lawson, who made certain that all her well-connected friends and her father's associates made it a point of wining and dining at Bottoms Up.

They'd been close for years, and when he'd grown tired of working for someone else and decided to pursue his dream of opening his own supper club, Dominique was behind him, pushing him along on those days when he didn't think it would work out. She'd even gone so far as to cosign the bank loan, and tossed in some extra cash to cover a few unexpected expenses which he'd since repaid. Even though she insisted that she didn't want it, Spence refused to be in debt to anyone, even to Dominique, who although was wealthy had her own money management issues due to impulsive spending.

Tonight's special was seared sea bass, hence the special sauce. He'd been offered money more times than he could count in exchange for sharing the ingredients with the world. He always teased the interviewers, saying that the secret was in the whisk.

He lifted pot covers, checked the refrigerators and pantries. Satisfied that his staff had everything under control, he went up front. Less than three hours remained before the dinner crowd would begin to arrive, and with Harry Connick, Jr., as the guest performer he would not leave anything to chance.

Michelle was just signing off on the shipment when Spence walked into the main dining room. She was giving instructions to one of the staff about the glassware.

Michelle Davis was a transplant from New York who had attended college in Louisiana and had never gone back home. They'd met while he was head chef at what was now his competitor's restaurant. She was the general manager. After a few drinks and a long night they fell into an on-again, off-again relationship, no strings, no commitment. An agreement that suited them both very well.

When Spence opened Bottoms Up, Michelle asked to work for him, and together they turned it into a showplace. Michelle's eye for layout and detail, along with her impeccable management skills, allowed Spence to breathe easy. Their sporadic relationship came to a mutual end when Michelle came to work at Bottoms Up.

Michelle tucked the inventory sheet into a folder on her clipboard just as Spence approached.

"Everything in order?"

She pressed the clipboard to her chest. Her brandy-toned eyes sparkled with excitement behind her designer frames. "The glasses are more exquisite than when we first picked them out."

"You mean when *you* picked them out."

Her sandy-brown face heated from beneath, giving it a toasted glow. "It would have been a joint effort if you had come shopping."

"You stick to shopping and running the club and I'll stick to cooking."

"Speaking of running the club." She lowered the clipboard and tucked a stray lock of shimmering auburn hair behind her ears. "The phone has been ringing off the hook for tonight's show. Nichole has had to turn folks down all morning. We may need to get extra security."

Spence nodded. "You're right. No sense in leaving things to chance. I'll take care of it. Anything else?"

"I think that covers it for now."

"Great. I'll make those calls."

"Oh, Spence…"

He stopped and turned. A thick, silky black brow rose in question.

"Is Dominique coming tonight?"

He caught the edge in her voice, but being a wise man, he chose to ignore it.

"If she does, she'll take her usual table."

She gave a short nod and went in search of the maître d'.

Spence walked away. He didn't know what it was with women. They had this sixth sense or something. The thing between him and Michelle was long over, even if they often teased each other about "the times we had." Yet anytime a woman came within sniffing distance of him, Michelle would get all… He didn't even know what to call it. And Dominique was often the same but for different reasons. Her rationale for the arched brow and tight lips when he introduced one of his dates was that she was only trying to look out for him. "Women can be quite cunning," she'd warn him, as if he didn't know. The two of them in the same space was like watching two panthers scope each other out. It was all very sleek and polite but potentially dangerous.

What he did hope, barring everything else, was that Desiree would come along with her sister, if the unpredictable Dominique decided to show up.

It had been a while since he'd seen Desiree. The few times that he'd stopped by the Lawson mansion with Dominique, Desiree had been out, and it had been months since she'd come to Bottoms Up for dinner.

Even though there was no doubt that Dominique and Desiree were identical twins, they were as different as night and day. Dominique was the storm. Desiree was the calm that followed. Although he and Dominique were never a couple—although they'd come really close—he often wondered how things would be if he'd met Desiree first.

For the moment he didn't have time to dwell on it. He had a big night ahead.

"How about I get you a date, Desi?" Dominique said as they sat on the pool deck, soaking in the last of the sun.

"I don't want you to get me a date. How about that?"

Dominique twisted around in the chair to look at her sister. "Why not?"

Desiree lifted her sunglasses from the bridge of her pert nose and glared at her twin. "Because I don't need you to get me a date. If I wanted one, I would have one," she said, struggling to control her temper. Patrice, her sister...everywhere she looked someone was trying to hook her up with somebody, as if she was some sort of hopeless spinster. Their older sister, Lee Ann, used to be able to run interference, but since her marriage and relocation to Washington with her husband, Desiree had been left on her own to fight off the onslaught.

"Look, I just want you to be happy."

"What makes you think I'm not happy?"

Dominique's confusion drew her thin brows together. "How can you be? I mean...women have needs, too, Desi," she said, lowering her voice as if someone else could hear.

The rims of Desiree's ears burned. She turned away. Dominique always knew what buttons to push intentionally or otherwise. She could count on one hand and still not reach five, the number of men she'd had in her bed—or whose bed she had been in. Dominique, however, was another story. She was the female version of their very notorious playboy brother, Rafe. Dominique changed men and relationships like nail polish. They were varied and often.

Dominique reached out and placed her hand on Desiree's arm. "I'm not saying that you're not happy.... It's just that I want you to have someone in your life...to look out for you, take you on great vacations, hot dates, massage your feet." She grinned and so did Desiree.

"I want those things, too, Dom, when the time and the person are right. These two things haven't lined up for me yet. But they will." She hoped but didn't say.

Dominique sighed. "Well, at least meet some of my friends."

"I know all of your friends," Desiree said drolly.

Dominique made a face, then suddenly brightened. "Hey, what about a dating service!"

Desiree held up her hand. "Oh, hell, no."

"Why not? Cyberdating, speed dating and all those blind dates are the rage." She leaned close. "I've done them all."

Desiree's eyes widened in surprise. "You're kidding."

Dominique shook her head. "Nope. And it's a blast." She reached for her frosted glass of mango juice and took a sip.

Desiree thought about it. Blind dates, speed dating, internet dating. What happened to dating the old-fashioned way? "Okay," she finally said on a breath.

Dominique sat up. "Okay...like okay, you'll do it?"

Desiree drew in a long breath. "Yes. But on one condition," she quickly added.

"Sure. Anything."

"Sixty days. That's it. If I don't find someone worthwhile in two months, then the deal is off and you will never utter another word to me about my love life again. Deal?"

Dominique pursed her lips in thought. Sixty days was not a lot of time. But if she couldn't find the perfect hot body to warm her sister's bed at night, then no one could.

"Deal." She lifted her glass.

Desiree touched her glass to Dominique's. "Deal. Sixty days and not a minute more."

"Fine. But I think this calls for a celebration."

"What kind of celebration?"

"Harry Connick, Jr., is at Spence's place tonight. Let's go."

Desiree's heart knocked at the sound of his name. "The place will be packed. We'll never get a seat."

"I always get a seat." She winked. "Don't even worry about it. So come on. Let's celebrate this new venture."

If she decided to go, she'd have a chance to see Spence. Not that it mattered. Spence had women all over him. Not only was he eye candy, but he was also charming and funny, talented and wealthy. She'd often wondered if Spence and Dominique had ever… If so, it was none of her business. "Sure. I don't have plans and I love Harry."

"Great." Dominique popped up. "I'll call Spence and tell him to hold my table. Show starts at ten!" She sauntered off toward the house.

Chapter 3

When Desiree and Dominique arrived at Bottoms Up, the line to get in wrapped around the block. Dominique pulled up to the valet.

"Evening, Ms. Lawson."

"Hi, Eddie. Big crowd tonight," she said, grabbing her purse. She exited the car and Eddie got in behind the wheel as Desiree got out.

"Just go right up front, Ms. Lawson," Eddie said before shutting the door.

"Thanks."

Desiree followed Dominique up to the front of the line, bypassing the waiting throng held at bay by a red velvet rope.

"Hey, Charles," Dominique greeted the bouncer.

Charles looked like a bear but was as gentle as a kitten. He was truly a testament to looks being deceiving.

He smiled when he saw her. "Good to have you with us tonight. And, Ms. Desiree, it's been a while."

"Good to see you, Charles."

"Come on in, ladies." His burly body made a path for them and they stepped inside, ignoring the grumbling at their backs.

Bottoms Up might have been billed as a supper club, but it certainly had an upscale nightclub feel. Two circular levels with multi-rows of tables allowed the seated guests to see the stage from any vantage point.

The decor was chic and avant-garde with smoked glass tables and chairs, muted recessed lighting, gleaming silver railings, mirrored walls, three bars and several private booths for larger groups. Between the dining tables were couches and lounge chairs and, of course, the menu was to die for.

The sisters stepped into the dim interior and were immediately met by the hostess, who took them to Dominique's reserved table.

Michelle was crossing the room and spotted them the moment they were seated. Her body tensed. *Not one, but two of them,* she thought to herself. Desiree, the other sister, wasn't really on her radar. She had always seemed nice whenever they had the chance to meet, and she was cordial, if not almost aloof, when she saw Spence. It was Dominique that was the fly in her ointment. She put on her happy face and walked over to their table.

"Good evening, ladies. Nice to see you both."

"Michelle, how are you?" Desiree offered a big smile.

Dominique glanced up. "Michelle." Her gaze did a

sixty-second inventory. "You put on a little weight. It looks good."

Michelle's jaw clenched. "I love the shoes. They add about what? Three inches to your height?" she said, taking her dig at Dominique's diminutive stature.

"So, great crowd tonight," Desiree said, jumping in before she became a casualty in the verbal catfight. "Harry can definitely draw the crowd."

Michelle drew in a breath and forced a smile. She turned to Desiree. "Yes, he can. We've reached capacity and it's still early. Well, you ladies have a great evening. Good seeing you."

"Oh, could you let Spence know we're here?" Dominique smiled sweetly.

Michelle turned away before she lost her manners and smacked the lip gloss right off of Dominique Lawson's mouth.

"What is wrong with you?" Desiree said from between clenched teeth. "You act like you're twelve every time you're around that woman."

Dominique rolled her eyes. "She irks my last nerve."

"I'm sure the feeling is mutual. But the both of you need to get over it. Whatever it is."

"She's jealous because of my relationship with Spence. She always has been and she wishes it was her."

So do I. Desiree sighed inwardly and turned her attention to the crowd.

Michelle wound her way around the tables and bodies until she reached the kitchen, where she was sure she would find Spence overseeing each and every dish. He had little tolerance for any slipups or shoddy service or improperly prepared meals. His cooks and servers were thoroughly screened and trained and he paid well for their time and talents. But he had no qualms about letting anyone go that could not live up to the standards that he'd set. He was a hard taskmaster, but his staff knew that above all else he was fair. Michelle admired him for that and everything else that made up Spence Hampton.

"Full house." Michelle eased up alongside him as he tasted the lobster bisque.

Spence took the wooden spoon and dropped it in the sink. He wiped his hands on his apron. "How are we doing outside?"

"Charles has started turning people away. We probably should have had two shows."

Spence shook his head. "One show, one night. It gives it that much more cachet to have been here." He winked at her, then crossed the wide, bustling kitchen, peeking over shoulders as he went. Michelle was close behind.

"The Lawson sisters are here."

Spence's step stuttered for a moment and Michelle bumped into his back.

"Oh, sorry."

"Did they get seated?" He continued walking.

"Yes. Dominique got her table."

He gave a short nod of his head. He checked his apron. "I'll go out and say hello."

Before Michelle could say another word, Spence had pushed through the swinging kitchen doors and stepped out into the main lounge. As she stood there, she wondered for the countless time what Dominique Lawson had that she didn't. In her heart she knew the answer but refused to accept it. One day she would have him back, once and for all, and she'd never have to think about Dominique Lawson with Spence ever again.

Michelle was right, Spence thought as he took in the capacity crowd. Every table was taken, the couches were full, the bar was lined from end to end and the waiters and waitresses were doing double time to keep up.

After a bit of maneuvering, he eased around the mezzanine floor and worked his way toward Dominique's table.

Desiree had her back to him, but he'd know that slender neck, the curve of her bare shoulders and those wild spiral cotton candy curls anywhere. Dominique, as usual, was busy charming the waiter, encased in a body hugging minidress that looked as if it was painted on. Spence smiled to himself as he approached.

"Ladies, ladies." He looked from one to the other.

Dominique beamed. Spence slipped his arm around her waist and she did the same as she kissed his rugged cheek.

Desiree watched the exchange, thankful for the muted light that hid the longing in her eyes. Looking at the two of them together, one could easily conclude from their body language that they were lovers. Her stomach tensed. She glanced away and concentrated on her apple martini while her sister teased and cooed with Spence. He towered over her sister. His slender but hard body slid along the lines of her sister's and she wished it was her. The deep chocolate of his smooth skin always made her hungry for what she knew would be sweetness, if she only got a chance to taste it.

"Desiree." The deep ripple of his voice vibrated down to her pedicured toes.

She casually glanced up and tumbled into the depths of his onyx eyes. "How are you, Spence?" The lighting played with the deep, dark waves of his closely cut hair.

"I can't complain. And to what do I owe the pleasure of your visit tonight?"

Desiree felt all fluttery inside. "You have Dominique to thank. She convinced me to come out tonight. And when she said Harry would be here…" She lifted one shoulder and smiled. Her deep dimples flashed.

"Whatever the reason, I'm glad you're here."

She refused to read more into what he said. "I'm looking forward to the show."

Spence took a step back. He was thankful that his face was hidden in the shadows that played around the room. It was silly of him to think that Desiree might have wanted to see him. In all the years that he'd known the sisters, Desiree had not once given him reason to think that they were anything more than acquaintances.

"Well, you ladies enjoy your evening. Whatever you need is yours."

"Thanks, sweetie," Dominique said. "If I don't see you later tonight, I'll give you a call during the week."

He nodded and walked off.

Dominique turned to her sister. "Are you okay? You seem distracted."

Desiree blinked and brought the room and her attention back into focus. "Yeah, just taking it all in."

"Spence has done an incredible job with this place, hasn't he?" She reached for her drink.

"Wonderful," Desiree said absently and wondered if she would see Spence again before the night was over. But what was the point, anyway? He had no interest in her, and for her to continue to daydream about the two of them together was a waste of valuable brain cells. Spence Hampton was off-limits and that was the end of it. She only wished that her heart was as reasonable as her head.

Spence continued to keep his focus on the menu and ensuring that his guests were all taken care of. Although that part of running Bottoms Up was Michelle's job, he always wanted to keep his hand in. He didn't want to be one of those owners that had no idea of what went on in their establishment.

Once Harry took the stage and the majority of the dinner guests had been served, he took a moment to relax. The tough part of the evening was over. He made his rounds of the tables and checked on his guests, seeing many familiar faces and plenty of new ones.

When he opened Bottoms Up, he had no idea that it would take off the way that it did, but his business was one of the premier locations in Baton Rogue and all the surrounding areas. He had much to be proud of.

The enthusiastic crowd kept Harry and his band onstage long after his set was supposed to be finished. But being the consummate entertainer, he had no intention of disappointing his fans, who clamored for "more, more."

By 2:00 a.m., the crowd was down to a few die-hard stragglers who were finishing up drinks or collecting numbers for potential rendezvous.

Spence took a look around, hoping to get a last glimpse of Desiree. Their table was empty.

"Thanks for coming, sis." Dominique yawned as she unlocked the door to their home.

"I'm glad I did. I had a great time." She pulled off her shoes and walked barefoot up the stairs.

"It's so different without Lee Ann around. Just a few months ago she would have been sitting in the living room, pretending to be reading but really waiting up for one of us to come home."

Desiree laughed. Their older sister, Lee Ann, was definitely the nurturing one of the family. She'd taken over the care of the family and the running of the household after their mother passed. But now that she was married to Preston, she finally had a life of her own. She was sorely missed.

"I'm actually tired," Dominique said, opening the door to her bedroom. "I must be getting old."

"You! I doubt that."

Dominique turned beneath the threshold of her door. She wagged a finger at her sister. "We still have a deal, right?"

Desiree drew in a breath and sighed. "Yes, we still have a deal."

"Great. Tomorrow is going to be the first day of your brand-new life. Just leave it to me."

"Night."

Dominique blew a kiss and closed her door.

Desiree continued down the hallway to her bedroom. Slowly getting undressed, she thought about her evening and how she had felt when she saw Spence. She'd made it a point to steer clear of him as much as possible. There was no point in window-shopping—seeing what you want in the window and knowing that you can't have it. Yet every time she saw him, the desire that she felt never lessened. If anything, her longing for him had only increased over the years. But truth be told, she didn't want to be one of many. Spence Hampton had a line of women whom he'd either dated or who were waiting in line to do so. As far as she knew, there had never been anyone serious in his life and not even Dominique had managed to slow him down.

She didn't fully understand their relationship, she mused as she slipped under the sheets and turned off the bedside lamp. There was no doubt in her mind that there was an intimacy between them. But she dared not ask. She didn't think she could stand to hear what she already knew.

Desiree lay on her back. Her eyes slowly adjusted to the dark. *Tomorrow is the first day of your brand-new life.* She flipped onto her side and shut her eyes.

It was nearly 4:00 a.m. and Spence still couldn't sleep, so he found himself in his garage with the overhead lights glaring and the shining insides of a 1978

Ford Mustang open for view. Had his passion for cooking not been stronger than his love of working on and restoring cars, he would have been in a completely different business.

His father was a mechanic, and when he was a kid growing up in Memphis, Spence spent many afternoons after school and during the summer watching his father work on cars in his small automotive shop. "If you have a trade, you'll never be without food on the table," his father used to always say. And growing up, he always assumed that he would be a mechanic like his father.

He'd been working on the Mustang for about two months. Every night, after closing the restaurant, he would come out to his garage and work on it. It was bright red, with a white leather interior. The body was fully restored and the engine purred like a satisfied kitten. But the soft sounds of the engine belied its truth. The Mustang could reach 120 miles per hour without a shudder.

The restored beauty would fetch a pretty penny if he ever decided to put it on the market, something that his best friend and film producer Dexter Beaumont tried to convince him to do.

Working on a car, to Spence, was akin to unlocking the mysteries of women, their fine lines, sleek and smooth bodies and the power that they possessed beneath their exterior.

He turned off the overhead lights. There wasn't anything else that he could do with her besides taking her out for a spin and opening her up. It was late, his mind said, but his body needed to release some of his pent up energy. He closed the hood and opened the driver's side door, got in behind the wheel and inserted the key. A touch of a button and the roof eased back; the engine purred softly beneath him. He put the car in gear and eased out of his garage and into the early morning.

The streets of Baton Rouge were still. A light breeze blew in the spring air. Lamplight joined with the starlight and the half-moon, giving the slow drive an almost surreal feel.

He knew these streets and back routes like he knew his own name. Although he wasn't a native of Louisiana, he had spent the better part of his life here and wouldn't trade it for anything.

Above the crest of the trees and homes the first pink rays of daylight began to spread across the inky sky, as if being slowly painted with the stroke of an artist's hand. He headed for the highway and once there he shifted gears, pressed on the accelerator and soon the city was no more than a tiny image in his rearview mirror.

He drove for more than an hour, relishing in the feel and power of the car. Driving usually relaxed him, took his mind off things he didn't want to think about. But not tonight. As much as he tried, he couldn't shake images of Desiree out of his head. On more than one occasion he'd started to talk to Dominique about her sister, but good sense had prevailed. For reasons that he couldn't put his finger on, he didn't think that it would sit very well with Dominique. She had her own impressions of him and teased him constantly about his parade of women. What she didn't know was that the parade was only a replacement for who he really wanted—Desiree Lawson.

He turned onto his street and pulled into his garage. Maybe it was time to do something about his unrequited feelings once and for all.

Chapter 4

Desiree had always known that her twin was determined and single-minded. However, she'd never been on the receiving end of all that focus, and in the first twenty-four hours of their pact, she was already regretting it.

"First I thought we could do some double-dating. Chris, a guy I met a few weeks ago on the tennis court, has some really great-looking friends," Dominique was saying while she sipped her orange juice.

Desiree groaned. "Dom, you make me sound like some kind of castoff." She pushed back from the kitchen island counter and walked to the sink.

"Okay, how about this? What if I just invite Chris and one of his friends over here? That way, no pressure, only a friendly gathering at the pool."

Inwardly, Desiree cringed. She must have been out

of her mind or truly desperate to have agreed to this. "Fine," she said on a breath of frustration.

Dominique clapped and hopped up from her stool. "I'll give Chris a call." She pranced out of the kitchen.

"Hey, sis, why the long face?"

Desiree glanced up to see her brother Justin en route to his favorite spot in the house—the refrigerator. Every time she looked at her handsome younger brother, she was reminded of their mom: they both shared the same open and welcoming countenance.

"Oh, just thinking about some issues at work. How is school going?"

He shrugged. "Easy semester. Just looking forward to graduation."

"It will be here before you know it. Do you think you're going to take the consulting job or the congressional aide position?"

"I'm still deciding. Both opportunities are great. I want to make the right decision." He took a carton of eggs and a package of bacon out of the fridge.

"You will." She smiled. "I have all the confidence in the world in you."

"Thanks. Man, I sure miss having Lee Ann around." He took the eggs and bacon to the stove and took down the frying pan from the hanging rack overhead. "She always had breakfast ready on Sunday morning."

"Yep, Lee Ann always had everything under control. We were spoiled."

"When is Grace coming back?"

"Hopefully soon, sweetie, and then things can get back to normal," she teased.

Grace Howard was their longtime housekeeper, who'd gone to her native home of Grenada for more than two months, leaving shortly after Lee Ann's wedding to take care of her ailing mother.

"She said her mother is much better and getting up and around."

"That's good. I mean, I wouldn't want her to leave her mother but she sure is missed around here." He lined up the bacon and the pan sizzled.

"Well, I will leave you to your cooking. See you later." She patted him on his broad shoulders and walked off.

Located on the ground floor of the sprawling mansion were two home offices, one that Desiree used and one that her father used when he was in town. Even though it was Sunday and she could have been lounging on the pool deck, there was paperwork that she wanted to go through to prepare for a community forum later in the week. Rezoning was a major issue in the parish and the residents wanted to have their say.

Just as she was settling down to work, the opening and closing of doors and the sound of voices drifted to her from the front of the house. Her heart tumbled. Pushing back from the desk, she crossed the room to the partially opened door.

Dominique's laughter floated to her, followed by the rugged baritone of Spence. A slow heat moved through her, even though all she could make out was the impression and resonance of his voice, not the words.

She held the frame of the door to keep her feet from

moving by the magnetic pull of him. He'd obviously come to see Dominique and placing herself in front of him for some trumped-up reason would only make her look ridiculous.

Drawing in a long breath of resolve, she shut the door and returned to her computer. She was determined to focus on the work at hand even as images of her and Spence together, with her body wrapped around his, continued to battle for control of her senses.

As Spence followed Dominique through the house, he took surreptitious looks around in the hopes of spotting Desiree. The house was relatively quiet aside from the faint sounds of music coming from one of the upstairs rooms, which he assumed was Justin.

"So to what do I owe this surprise?" Dominique asked, leading the way to the back patio.

"I decided to take the Mustang for a ride and wanted who else but my best girl in the passenger seat."

"You're just the sweetest," she cooed, turning to him and lifting up on her toes to plant a kiss on his cheek. Her warm brandy-toned eyes moved slowly over his face. She used her thumb to gently wipe the lipstick from his cheek.

Why couldn't this be Desiree? he thought, taking her hand and kissing the inside of her palm. "Are you game?"

"When have I ever not been game?" She flashed him a wicked smile. "Let me run up and change. Make yourself at home. You know where everything is." She darted off and left Spence on the patio.

He walked over to the railing and looked out onto the expansive lawn. The Lawsons lived well, he mused. They were part of the elite of Louisiana. Yet, each member of the Lawson clan was as ordinary as the next person. None of them were known for lauding their family name and using their clout to get what they wanted. They worked hard in their chosen fields and didn't look for a free ride, although their name provided entrée into any door that they wanted opened.

The sound of the sliding door opening behind him turned him in that direction. His nostrils flared as he drew in a short breath.

"Hey," said Desiree.

"Hey, yourself. I didn't know you were here," he answered.

"Tucked away in my office. Last-minute stuff. I thought I heard a car pull up."

"Yeah, I brought over the Mustang, which I'd been working on. Came to see if Dom wanted to go for a ride."

"Hmm." She glanced at her sandals for a moment. "Well, you guys enjoy yourself. I'm going to get back to work. Good to see you."

She started to close the door.

"How did you like the show last night? I didn't get to see you afterward."

She was half in the door. "It was great. I had a wonderful time and, of course, the dinner was superb." She smiled. "I dreamed about you—it all night." Her face burned. Why did she say that?

"So did I...I mean, I have these crazy dreams sometimes before a big...event."

She leaned against the door frame. "You don't strike me as someone who gets...lets things get you all worked up...sleepless." Oh, God, she was babbling.

Spence gripped the railing behind him to keep from walking right up to her and taking her in his arms the way he'd been dreaming about when he finally did fall asleep. "You'd be surprised."

"I'm sure I would."

"You should come more often."

The air stuck in her chest. She knew good and well what he meant but her libido had taken charge. "Come?"

"To the club."

She ran her tongue lightly across her lips. "I don't get out as much as I should."

"All work?"

"Something like that." She ran her hand absently along the door frame. "Especially with the elections coming up and all of the local referendums." She finally felt the floor beneath her feet again, having moved the topic to something that she could manage.

"Yeah, the whole rezoning thing," he said, nodding his head as he spoke. "I've been following you—it, in the papers."

Her eyes widened ever so slightly in pleasant surprise. "A very hot topic for the community. The rezoning will bring business but at the expense of much needed housing."

"There has to be a middle ground," he said, his expression tightening in thought. "I know from experience the good, the bad and the ugly about gentrification."

"Experience?"

He nodded. "Back in Memphis, where I grew up, the same thing happened. City claimed eminent domain and ran a highway through the neighborhood, pushed people out and built a mall." He expelled a mirthless laugh.

"I'm sorry, that must have been horrible. How old were you?"

"Hmm, 'bout fifteen. Old enough to be angry, but not old enough to do much about it."

"What did your family wind up doing?"

"They gave my mother some money for our place." He glanced off, back to that unsettling time in his life. "We moved into a walk-up apartment in a three-family house."

In all the years that she'd known Spence this was all a revelation. She knew he wasn't born in Louisiana but had no idea that Memphis was home or that he was raised by a single mom. Desiree watched the montage of emotions crease his brow, tighten his casual body language and put a hard edge in his voice. That experience, she sensed, changed him somehow. Forced him to see the injustices of life, perhaps too soon.

Spence blew out a breath and returned from that place he'd put behind him and smiled at Desiree. He opened his mouth to speak just as Dominique appeared behind her sister. Desiree stepped out of the way.

"Good seeing you, Spence. Enjoy the ride!" She gave a short wave and walked away.

Dominique slid her sunglasses on her nose. "Ready?"

"Sure."

He walked alongside Dominique as they rounded the house from the back to reach his car on the driveway.

"She sure is a beauty." Dominique ran her hand along the high-glossed side.

Spence glanced at the house and could have sworn he saw someone drop the curtain in the window. "Yeah, she is."

Desiree turned away from the window, mortified at the thought that she might have been caught staring. She felt as if he'd looked right at her—*or through her.* Why did she even care? He hadn't come to see her. He'd come to see her sister. He never even asked if she wanted to come along. Why should he? She would have just been a third wheel.

She pushed out a long breath. Yes, Patrice and Dominique were right. It was time she got a life and put a man in it. She reentered her office and shut the door behind her.

"Where are we headed?" Dominique asked, leaning back against the cool leather as the warm Louisiana wind blew around them. She rested her elbow against the frame of the open window.

He should have asked Desiree to come along. Although he was pretty sure she would have said no. She'd never seemed interested in whatever he and Dominique might be doing together, whether it was a day at the shore, going out for drinks with friends…parties. She always had "other plans," which was why he was so surprised to see her last night. And seeing her had only stirred up all the desires he'd kept under a lid. She was the real reason he'd come to the Lawson home in the first place.

"Are you listening to me?"

"Huh?" He snatched a glance in Dominique's direction.

She pursed her lips in feigned annoyance. "I asked you where we were going. If you don't have any place special in mind, I want to pop by and see Rafe for a minute. Is that okay?"

"Yeah, sure. Not a problem."

"Is something wrong?"

"No. Why?"

"You seem distracted or out of it."

He chuckled. "Naw. I'm good." He turned to her and winked.

She cut him a look from the corner of her eye, studying his stiff profile, which was so out of character. Spence was usually so laid-back and relaxed, always an easy smile on his face. But today his entire body was tight and inflexible. He barely looked at her, and when he did, it was as if he didn't really see her. And *that* was something she certainly wasn't used to. She ran her fingers through her short, spiky hairdo and wondered what was really on Spence's mind.

"How's the new program going at the agency?"

Dominique shot him a look. "Oh, you're talking to me now?"

"What's that supposed to mean?"

"I might as well not even be here for all the attention you've paid to me since I got in the car."

"Now you're being silly."

Her neck jerked back. "Silly?"

"Yes, silly."

She folded her arms tightly beneath her breasts and pouted.

Spence inhaled deeply. He and Dominique had been close for years. He'd grown accustomed to her moods and her often irrational feelings of being ignored. It had taken him a long time to understand that it wasn't him or anything that he was or wasn't doing; it was pure insecurity on her part. At times it could be endearing, and he'd want to comfort her and make it all go away; other times it was totally frustrating. He knew it was why she was always flamboyant, the party girl, the one who needed to be noticed. And when she wasn't, she pouted, like now.

"So are you going to tell me how the program is going, or are you going to keep those luscious lips poked out until we get to Rafe's house? My mama always said, 'If you do your mouth like that, your lips are gonna stay that way,'" he said in a bad falsetto with a heavy Southern twang.

Dominique turned to look at him and rolled her eyes and tried not to laugh.

"It's going fine. Thank you very much for asking."

Dominique was the executive director of First Impressions, a nonprofit agency that provided clothing and training to disadvantaged women and single mothers.

She'd recently been approved for a grant to fund a GED program.

"How many students so far?"

"Can you believe we already have a waiting list?" She shook her head in wonder.

"Yeah, actually I can. Lotta people are struggling out there, Dom. All they need is a chance."

She nodded thoughtfully. "I don't think I ever realized how much until I started the agency."

"You do good work." He turned to her. "I'm proud of you."

She reached across the gears and squeezed his hand as the car drew to a stoplight. "Thanks. That means a lot coming from you." Her eyes held his for a moment.

He turned his attention back to the road. "Rafe's town house is on the next street, right?"

"Yep. Third one from the corner, on the left."

"Does he know you're coming?"

"No."

"Dom, suppose he's…busy."

She chuckled. "What else would be new?"

"I've been trying to get him to come down to the club and play. He's always busy," Spence said, pulling into Rafe's driveway.

Dominique got out of the car and shut the door. "You should've told me. I would have spoken to him for you. Rafe can never tell me no."

They stood in front of the door. Spence turned to her. "Who can?"

Chapter 5

The house was too quiet. Justin had gone out with friends earlier and Dominique had yet to return. The rooms began to echo in Desiree's mind, highlighting her growing feeling of loneliness. Today would have been a perfect day to take a spin around the track, work out some of the kinks and get her mind wrapped around something that she could actually control. But Sundays were reserved for competitions only and she was not a competitive driver. At least not yet.

Restless, she went into the kitchen. Next to driving and reading, cooking was her passion. She decided to make jambalaya and went in search of the ingredients. While she gathered her ingredients and seasonings, she turned on the small television to her favorite cable channel— The Food Network.

As she cut and sliced sausage, deveined the shrimp

and chopped green and red peppers, a smile came to her lips and she felt a rush of warm memories of the many hours she'd spent at her mother's side, watching with fascination as she prepared a meal. She could almost see her mother standing next to her, watching in approval.

The ringing phone jarred her away from the warm but melancholy thoughts. She wiped her hands on her apron and picked up the phone from the counter.

"Lawson residence."

"Hey, sis, I meant to tell you before I darted out that I called Chris and he's going to stop by later this evening, around six, and he's bringing his friend Maxwell. I thought we could have a few drinks, something light to eat and chat…."

"Dom! How could you do something like that without telling me first? Did it occur to you that I might have something to do?"

"Do you?"

"That's not the point," Desiree tossed back, her anger boiling over. "This is so typical of you."

"What's that supposed to mean?"

"It means that you have tunnel vision. You think the whole world revolves around you and your wants. And it doesn't!"

"Rafe is coming," she said in her sweetest voice to try to smooth things over. She knew how close Desiree was to Rafe. She could almost see the tight line between her sister's eyes begin to ease.

Desiree pushed out a breath. Seeing her brother would

do her a world of good, even if she was pissed off with her sister.

"Don't you dare tell Rafe about this friend of yours, Dominique, or I swear our deal is off and I'll never speak to you again. Understood?"

"All right, all right. I won't breathe a word." She smiled with triumph. "Um, you want me to pick up anything while I'm out?"

Desiree squeezed her eyes shut and shook her head. Her sister was truly a piece of work. "A couple of rolls of French bread. I am making jambalaya. Guess I'll have to make some extra."

"Oh, that's my favorite! I'll bring some wine, too."

"Hmm."

"See you later."

Before she could ask if Spence was with her, Dominique had disconnected the call.

Dominique returned to the living room, where Spence and Rafe were talking about Rafe coming to play at Bottoms Up. She stood between them. "Hey, just got off the phone with Desi. Guess what? She's fixing her specialty and wanted to have some folks over."

"Tonight?" Rafe asked.

"Yeah, around six. Bring a date." She turned to Spence. "You can come, too. Bring someone. It'll be fun."

The two men looked at each other.

"I'm always up for a free meal. Next to you, my sister is a damned good cook," Rafe said over a light chuckle.

"And I'm sure I can find some hungry young lady to be my escort."

"What about you, Spence?" Dominique asked.

"Hmm, I don't know. I had plans to make this an early night."

"It will be. Come on," she cooed, bending down in front of him. She ran her finger along his jaw.

He hesitated. It would give him a chance to spend some time in Desiree's company. "Okay. Just for a little while."

Dominique popped up. "Great." She looked at her watch. It was almost two. "Can you drop me at the market before you take me back? I promised Desi I'd get some French bread and a couple of bottles of wine."

Spence pushed up from his seat. "I'm apparently at your disposal."

Rafe chuckled. "Yes, my darling sister does have a way of manipulating people."

"That's a terrible thing to say about your own sister," replied Dominique.

"What would you call it?" Rafe asked while he walked them to the front door.

"Hmm, the power of positive persuasion," she said.

"Riiight," Spence and Rafe chorused.

Dominique tossed her head and sashayed out. "See you tonight, Rafe." She finger waved.

"Later, man," Spence said, shaking Rafe's hand. "I'm gonna hold you to coming down next month."

Rafe bobbed his head. "We'll work it out. Take care of my crazy sister."

"Always."

"See you in a few."

Desiree had been trained well by her mother, Louisa, and her sister, Lee Ann, on how to put a dinner party together, from small gatherings to full-out banquets, but it never got easier. Like her mother and sister, Desiree was a perfectionist.

After putting the jambalaya on to simmer, she prepared the ingredients for dirty rice and fixed a huge tossed salad. She chilled the only bottle of wine in the house, and cut up exotic cheeses and mixed a bowl of spinach dip that her brother Rafe loved.

With all the preparations done, she went out back to check on the seating by the pool and to stock the ice chest with water, beer and soda. Since the dinner would be totally buffet style, she set out the dishes, cutlery and glasses on the granite counter in the kitchen. *Every man for himself,* she thought, taking out the linen napkins and placing them on the counter. She took a quick look around at her handiwork. Satisfied, she lowered the flame on the pot and darted upstairs to find something to wear and take a shower.

She didn't like this whole blind date thing, she thought as she stood beneath the relaxing spray of water. What if he was a real jerk and she was forced to play nice all evening? She groaned. She should have never let Dominique talk her into this. But a deal was a deal. She would have to make the most of it.

* * *

"Need some help?" Dominique asked from the other side of the kitchen door.

Desiree was taking the citronella candles down from the cabinet. "You think you can manage to light these?"

As usual, Dominique had made herself scarce the instant she'd returned home, leaving everything up to Desiree to handle.

"Fine, but you get the door. It's probably Chris and his friend Max. I can't be in two places at once." She took the tray that held the six glass-enclosed candles and went out back.

Desiree forced herself not to scream and went to the front door. She put on her best smile, took a breath and opened the door.

"Spence!" She looked from Spence to Michelle. Her heart thundered.

"You look surprised," said Spence.

"No...not at all. I... Come in. Michelle, it's good to see you again."

"We brought dessert." Michelle held up a bag that contained a gallon tub of raspberry sorbet.

"I'll take that. Thanks so much. We're out back. Spence, you know the way."

Desiree swallowed over the dry knot in her throat as she watched them walk toward the backyard, still held in place by shock.

"Something sure smells good."

She turned back toward the opened door and felt a

brief moment of calm when she saw her brother Rafe.
For an instant she wanted to simply rest her head on his
chest. She opened her arms instead. "Hey, sweetie." She
hugged him tight, then stepped back.

"Desiree, this is Crystal. Crystal, my sister Desiree."

Crystal stuck out her hand, which Desiree shook.
"Nice to meet you."

"You, too. Please come in." She shut the door and slid
her arm around her brother's waist. "How ya doing?"

"Good. Better," he said quietly.

Mere weeks before Lee Ann's wedding to Preston,
Rafe had taken a real dive. He'd gone on a drinking binge
and got himself pretty banged up riding his motorcycle.
They'd all been worried about him. Rafe was always so
carefree and invincible, for lack of a better word, and
to see him the way he had been gave them all pause.
The volatile relationship between Rafe and their father,
Branford, had been at the root of it. It had taken a lot
of years to get to where it was and it was going to take
time to mend it.

Dominique came floating out into the foyer with
an empty bottle of wine in her hand. Her expression
brightened when she saw Rafe.

"There's my handsome brother." She sauntered up to
him and kissed his cheek, then focused her attention on
the woman on his arm. "I'm Dominique."

"Crystal Blanchette."

Dominique gave her a quick once-over, taking in her
sleek shoulder-length hair, long neck and slinky body,
which was wrapped in a scoop-necked aqua sheath that

outlined every curve and barely hit her knees to display her dancer's legs. All her brother's lady friends were the same type: they were tall and statuesque and looked as if they'd fallen off of a fashion magazine cover. She wouldn't last, either. None of them did.

"Well, do make yourself comfortable, Crystal. We're just getting set up out back," said Dominique.

We, Desiree thought, not at all amused.

Dominique turned to Desiree after Rafe and Crystal headed to the backyard. "Where does he find them?" she said under her breath. "And why in the hell did Spence bring that woman with him?"

Desiree drew in a breath. "Dominique, this was your brilliant idea. Now live with it!" She strode off toward the kitchen to check on dinner. She lifted the cover on the jambalaya and it rattled all over the top of the pot. Her hand shook. The last person she expected to see was Spence, and then to see him with another woman, even though it was Michelle, was a bit more than she was prepared for. She squeezed her eyes shut. This was going to be a long night.

"I'll get it," she heard her sister sing out in time to the ringing of the front doorbell.

"Need some help?"

She gasped and dropped the cover on the floor.

"Didn't mean to scare you." Spence leaned down and picked up the cover, took it to the sink and washed it off before he handed it back to Desiree. He angled his head to the side. "You okay?"

"Yes." She swallowed and forced a smile. "I'm fine.

You know how these things are. You want everything to be just right."

"Mind if I take a peek?"

"Sure."

He lifted the cover on the jambalaya, then took the wooden spoon and dipped it into the tempting ingredients. He brought the steamy mixture to his lips and took a taste.

Desiree held her breath.

"Incredible," he finally uttered. He washed off the spoon. "Better than mine."

Desiree sputtered a nervous laugh. "You're just saying that."

"I wish I was. It's the combination of spices." His gaze moved slow and lazy across her face. "You'll have to teach me the—"

"There you are. I just can't get my sister to sit down. Desi, this is Chris and his friend Max DeLaine. Max, my sister Desiree."

Max crossed the short space and took Desiree's hand. "My pleasure. Your sister has been singing your praises."

"Has she?" Desiree took in Max's warm butterscotch complexion, which was the perfect palette for his light brown eyes and dark brown hair. Nice height and build. His semi-casual outfit, a light gray sports jacket with dark slacks and an open-collared white shirt, looked good on him from head to toe. And she could tell from the moment he took her hand that he was entirely not her type.

Dominique linked her arm through Chris's and

then Spence's. "Come on, fellas. Let me fix you two a drink."

Spence gave Desiree a parting smile and followed Dominique and Chris out of the kitchen. She wanted to fall through the floor. But her mother, God rest her soul, would be completely disappointed.

Instead she began ladling the jambalaya into two huge chafing dishes and set them out on the counter. "So, Dominique told you about me, but she didn't tell me about you."

He leaned against the counter while she prepared the buffet.

"I teach over at Southern University."

She turned to him. "Really?"

He grinned and his eyes picked up the lights and sparkled.

"You look surprised."

She glanced away. "I am."

"Why?"

She searched her mind for an inoffensive answer. "My sister travels in some interesting circles, but not usually with college professors."

He folded his arms across his chest and chuckled. "I see. But what about you?"

She took the salad from the fridge. "What do you mean?"

"What kind of circles do you travel in?"

"Very small ones," she said, laughing lightly.

He took the bowl from her hand and placed it on the counter. "I doubt that. The Lawsons don't have small circles."

She'd heard the sound before, the tap-tap at opportunity's door. She let out a breath of disappointment.

"Something wrong?"

"No. Not at all. So what do you teach at Southern?"

"Art history."

Her brows rose. "Really?"

"Again you look surprised."

She turned to the stove and began taking the dirty rice out of the pot and putting it into a chafing dish. She angled her body halfway toward him. "I had it in my mind that you teach high finance or economics."

He lowered his head a moment and chuckled. "I hated both of those subjects in school. I always leaned toward the arts, even as a kid. My father still hasn't accepted it. He was sure I was going to follow in his rather big footsteps."

And that was when it hit her. *DeLaine. DeLaine Enterprises.* His father was Beau DeLaine, who owned the DeLaine hotel chain, not to mention a string of ships that imported and exported goods to and from the gulf.

"I can understand why." She smiled softly. The irrational edge she'd felt toward him began to smooth out. At least he was his own man, she conceded. He could have taken the easy road and carried on the family tradition, but he'd opted for doing what he loved. She had to admire that. "So, tell me, what is your favorite art period...?"

Spence glanced up when Desiree appeared in the doorway to the patio, smiling brightly and laughing at whatever it was that the Max character had to say. She looked happy and completely captivated. A knot grew in the center of his stomach while he watched Max place his hand at the small of her back as she stepped across the threshold. His jaw clenched. He got up and plucked an icy cold bottle of Coors from the ice chest, twisted off the cap and took a long, cooling swallow. His eyes never left Desiree and Max as they worked side by side setting out the food in chafing dishes.

Michelle tried to pretend that she was interested in the debate between Rafe and Chris on the greatest saxophonists of all time, but her eyes and thoughts kept shifting back to Spence, who had looked like he was ready to implode from the moment he'd come back from the kitchen and sat down. Now he was zeroed in on Desiree and her date. Did Spence know the guy from somewhere? Had they had words at some point? And if not, why did Spence seem so focused on him? Her thoughts skipped a beat. Or was it Desiree?

The possibility made her hand shake, causing the contents of her glass to spill over the rim onto the table.

"Oh, clumsy me," she sputtered, reaching for a napkin and nearly knocking over Dominique's drink in the process. "So sorry." She wiped up the spill.

"No problem. There's plenty more where that came from." Dominique chuckled while Michelle cringed inside.

"Here, I'll take that," Spence offered, apparently coming out of his staring spell.

He took the wet napkin out of Michelle's hand and

got up. Michelle watched him bypass the first trash can to go to the one at the end of the serving table, where Desiree and Max were standing.

Desiree turned her full attention on Spence and Michelle had the stunning stabbing sensation that she'd been worried about the wrong sister all along.

Chapter 6

No one could have been happier than Desiree when the impromptu dinner party came to a merciful end. The tension at points had been as thick as the oil slicks that covered parts of the wetlands. Between Dominique's catty remarks about Michelle and Rafe's date, Crystal; Spence's weird behavior; Maxwell's wanting to get to know her better and Michelle's sudden bouts of clumsiness—she counted four incidents—Desiree felt as if she should have taken referee lessons instead of racing lessons. More than once she'd wanted to simply tell everyone to "go to your corners or go home," whatever worked.

Her head was pounding as she stood in the doorway, saying good-night to Max as she pulled out all the stops to remain the gracious hostess.

"I hope we get to see each other again," Max was saying over the thumping in her brain.

"That would be nice."

"Great. So, it's cool if I give you a call, say, next week?"

"Sure."

His light brown eyes lingered on her face for a moment. "Well, good night. I had a great time. Fabulous dinner."

She pushed a smile across her mouth. "Good night. Drive safe."

Maxwell nodded and trotted down the front steps to the path that led to the driveway.

Desiree released a long breath of weariness and slowly shut the door behind her. Spence had left a bit earlier with Michelle and had barely said good-night, which was so unlike him, and Michelle, although cordial, had looked as if she'd swallowed something bitter. Her lips had gone from lush to one thin line.

Rafe, as always, had sailed above the fray and had kept everyone entertained with his ribald jokes, and he'd even played a few numbers on one of his saxophones that he kept handy in the study. He strolled in from the back with his arm tucked securely around the waist of Crystal, who was gazing up at him adoringly. *They all do,* Desiree thought, mildly amused. *Poor girl. Another one to fall under Rafe Lawson's spell.*

"You did a wonderful job, Cher," he said. Rafe always used the endearment when he was pleased with her. "Mama woulda been proud." He gave her a wink.

Desiree stuck out her hand. "Good to meet you, Crystal. Make sure he treats you right."

"You wound me, Cher. Here you are, giving Crystal the wrong idea." He flashed that Lawson smile, and all was right with the world.

"Drive safely, Rafe," Desiree warned as the couple stepped outside.

"Yes, ma'am," he said, waving to her over his head.

Finally, Desiree closed the door after the last guest. Her darling twin had actually had the nerve to sneak out with Chris, leaving her with the task of being hostess, even if the whole evening was Dominique's idea.

Desiree returned to the back patio and cleaned up the remaining plates and cups, which were few. At least her guests had straightened up after themselves, she thought as she turned out the lights on the ground floor and slowly walked upstairs. It was nearly ten and she had a full day ahead of her tomorrow. With local elections taking place in a little more than a month, she had plenty to keep her busy at the office.

Desiree slid down into the steamy ylang-ylang-scented water, leaned back against the headrest in the extra-deep Jacuzzi tub and turned on the jets. She closed her eyes and let the rushing water massage the kinks out of her body. The soothing aroma wafted around her. She sighed and inhaled deeply. She wasn't sure if it was pure annoyance or fatigue that had her so out of sorts. Her plan for her Sunday had been totally disrupted by her self-indulgent sister. She had always wondered what it was like to simply float through life with the only concern being yourself. She flexed her toes and stretched her legs.

That was mean. Dominique was a victim of tunnel vision. When she set her mind on something, that was it. Which was a great attribute to have. The problem with Dom was that she had this unrealistic impression that her wants were everyone else's, as well.

She sighed. That wasn't what was really bothering her. She was used to Dom's impulsiveness invading her life. She reran the evening through her head in slow motion. Letting the events, bits of conversation and people flow through her until she got that funny feeling in the center of her stomach. It was a little trick she'd taught herself in her teens. When she had a sense that something was wrong or was about to happen to someone she cared about, she'd give her emotions a litmus test until she hit the right one. She relaxed her body. The call from Dominique about the surprise dinner party? No. Being set up with Max? A slight twinge but that wasn't it. Seeing Rafe and Crystal? Nope. Spence and Michelle? There it was. That funny feeling in her stomach. But she knew it was more than that. She'd known Michelle for ages and Spence even longer. They were business partners. He probably had thought nothing of inviting Michelle to join them for dinner.

She frowned. What else? What was it? Then she remembered. She'd been standing at the serving table and Spence approached. She'd turned to speak to him and happened to catch a look coming from Michelle that stunned her. She thought she'd imagined seeing that look of fury tightening Michelle's eyes and pinching her lips. It was quick, like a flash of lightning. There and gone. She remembered actually flinching for a second.

What could Michelle have against her? She knew that Michelle and Dominique were always at odds, but her relationship with Michelle had always been cordial.

Maybe there was something going on between Spence and Michelle, and Michelle was staking out her territory. The feeling settled like bad food in the center of her stomach.

She turned off the jets. If what she suspected was true, then that was even more reason for her to steer her thoughts as far away from Spence Hampton as possible.

She pushed up out of the tub, took her bath towel down from the hook and wrapped it tightly around her body, tucking the ends above the swell of her breasts. Padding into her adjoining bedroom, she finished drying and smoothed her body with shea butter, then slipped in between the cool sheets.

If Max did call her, she decided, she would go out with him. She would have to start somewhere, she conceded, and Max was nice enough, intelligent and good-looking. She yawned. Maybe with a little bit of time and patience on her part, he could become "her type."

She reached for the switch on the bedside lamp, turned it off and snuggled down under the covers. Yes, she would go out with Max. It was her last conscious thought before drifting off to sleep, but in her dreams her date was with Spence.

* * *

"So what did you think about Max?" Dominique asked, all smiles and dimples, when she crossed paths with her sister in the kitchen the following morning. She took a beignet from the tray on the island counter and dropped her oversize Birkin tote at her feet. She swung her curvy hips up on the stool.

Desiree shrugged. She poured a glass of orange juice. "He seems nice."

"Nice! He's a great guy, Desi."

"I'm sure he is," she said, noncommittal, hoping that her face didn't give away what was going on inside of her. Her hand shook ever so slightly. All night long she'd been on a merry-go-round of dreams of Spence that spanned the spectrum from warm and platonic to sensual, heart-stopping, erotic, to outright rated triple X. She couldn't shake them and it made her edgy and tingly at the same time.

"Are you okay?"

Desiree's head snapped up from staring into her juice. She focused on her sister and forcibly pushed away the image of draping her legs across Spence's back an instant before his sweet lips tasted hers.

"I'm fine. A little tired, that's all."

Dominique stared at her twin for a moment. She always knew when Desi was lying and it was obvious that she was lying now. Why, she had no clue. She checked her watch. And now she didn't have the time to squeeze it out of her or she would be late for work. She finished off her beignet, wiped her glossed lips and hopped down from the stool. "If you say so," she said, tossing her napkin in the trash and placing her plate in the dishwasher. "I have to run. Monday morning staff meeting." She made a face of discontent. She started to head out, then turned back and stopped. "Thanks for last night. You did a great job. And I'm really sorry if I put too much on you." She came over and kissed her sister's cheek, then removed the lip gloss smudge with the pad of her thumb. "Love ya." She spun away and headed out.

Desiree shook her head and smiled. Dominique always knew what to say and when to soften up your heart. You had to love her, tunnel vision and all.

Michelle was seated behind the desk in the back office, going over the inventory, when Spence walked in.

"Good morning."

"Morning. I didn't think you'd be here so early today." He hung his lightweight gray jacket on the hook behind the door.

"Hmm, just wanted to get a step ahead." She took in the hard lines of his chest beneath the fitted black T-shirt before looking away.

"Thanks for coming last night."

She glanced up. "I had a nice time." She smiled.

He walked over and sat on the edge of the desk. The heady scent of the African musk oil that he used short-circuited her thoughts. It took her a minute to realize that he'd asked her a question.

She blinked and cleared her throat. "Oh, I'm double-checking the orders for this week against what we have in stock. I want to make sure that the deliveries scheduled for later in the week won't have to be moved up. Business has been crazy lately."

Spence chuckled and her stomach did a slow dance. "I know. And in these tight times to say that your business is so busy that we have to worry about keeping up is saying something." He focused on her. "I owe a lot of that to you, Michelle. You have a handle on this business and I couldn't run it without you."

Her face heated. "Thanks. We're a team. None of this would have happened without all of us doing our part."

"You're right." He got down. "And I better get busy doing my part, before the lunch crowd gets only bread and water."

She watched him go and her thoughts drifted back to the night before, when he'd brought her home. They'd stood outside of her door, talking briefly, and when the inevitable silence fell between them, she was certain that he was going to kiss her. Her heart began to race. The anticipation made her feel as if her heart would burst from her chest. He cupped her chin in his palm. She held her breath. "Good night. Thanks for riding shotgun." He'd smiled before turning away and getting back into his car, and her insides had wilted like a plant that had gone too long without water.

Michelle put down her pen and slid her designer frames from her slender nose and set them down next to the inventory sheets. What was it going to take to make Spence notice she was more than just a business partner? And what was so special about those damned

Lawson women? She wouldn't soon forget the way Spence looked at Desiree as if he couldn't wait to take her to bed.

That was the way she wanted him to look at her, with raw desire and passion and lust and…

The knocking on the door jarred her from her reverie. "Yes…come in."

"Hey, Michelle." Jillian, one of the waitresses, poked her head in. "There's a delivery up front. You want me to take care of it?"

"Which one?"

"The cases of greens and tomatoes."

Michelle opened the order book and flipped to the vegetable section. She popped open the binder and took out the sheet. She handed it to Jillian. "Check the delivery against the sheet. Make sure they open the crates before you sign."

"Sure." Jillian took the sheet and left.

Michelle sighed deeply and closed the binder. In her ideal world she would do it all, handle the orders, manage the finances, develop and confirm deliveries, promote the restaurant and book the guests. Make herself indispensable. But Spence didn't believe in one-man shows. In his mind, all his staff must be cross-trained—with the exception of the cooks—so that they could pinch-hit if the need arose.

Of course, it made logical sense, Michelle conceded. It was the best way to run a successful business and keep your staff motivated. But it didn't have to make her happy. She got up from her seat and went out to check on Jillian.

* * *

"We need to have some security in place at the venue for the town hall meeting on Wednesday," Desiree was saying to her assistant, Valerie, as they went down the checklist of items. "Tempers are high over the rezoning and I want to be prepared."

"I'll make a call to Chief Duquaine. I'm sure he can spare us a couple of officers."

Valerie Ford was a political science graduate student at Xavier University. Even though she was an intern, she couldn't work harder if she was paid a six-figure salary. Desiree only wished that Valerie would stay on when she finished her degree.

Desiree nodded. "The next thing on the agenda is the local elections, and then state."

"The mudslinging is well on its way," Valerie said, tongue in cheek.

"Unfortunately, it will only get worse before it gets better." She flipped through some notes. "We're going to be handling the logistics for the city council hearings."

Valerie made a note. "How's your sister Lee Ann making out on Capitol Hill with her new husband?"

Desiree smiled. "She's settling in. She says she misses home, but she and Preston will be back during recess. She's working as a political consultant and she loves what she does, especially because she can be close to Preston."

"That must really be great to find someone who shares the same kinds of passions that you do."

"Yes," Desiree said, an absent note in her voice. What would her and Spence's shared passion be?

Valerie got up. "I'll start making those calls and see how many officers Duquaine can provide."

Desiree nodded. "Thanks." She leaned back in her seat just as her phone rang. "Office of the City Council, Desiree Lawson speaking."

"Your voice is as wonderful as I remember."

Desiree frowned. She really hoped this wasn't some nutty constituent. "I'm sorry…. What is your name and how can I help you?"

"No, I'm sorry. I shouldn't have assumed you'd recognize my voice. This is Max. Maxwell DeLaine."

Her face flamed. "Oh, I am so sorry. Hello. How are you?"

"No need to apologize. I know you're probably very busy, so I won't bend your ear." He paused a beat. "I was hoping that you'd consider having dinner with me… tomorrow night."

Desiree blinked rapidly. "Tomorrow?" she stammered.

"Too soon?"

"Uh…no. It's just…"

"I know it's a weeknight, but I promise to make it early."

She released a silent breath. *Tomorrow. Dinner. What the hell. Why not?* "Sure. Tomorrow sounds fine. I should be finished here around six."

"Perfect. I'll make reservations and I'll pick you up at six."

"Umm, just let me know where to meet you. Since I drive into work, I'll already have my car."

"Whatever works for you. As soon as I make the reservations, I'll give you a call. Do you have any preferences?"

"I'll leave that up to you."

"No problem. I'll give you a call later this afternoon."

"Fine."

"Have a good day."

"You, too." She slowly hung up the phone. *A date. Hmm.* Well, she'd decided she had to start somewhere. She was going to put all her misgivings aside, open her mind and enjoy herself.

Chapter 7

Spence stirred the steaming pot of crawfish, then turned to the counter behind him to begin preparing the seasonings that he would add later. The crawfish were another of his signature dishes, always in demand. Cooking or driving tended to relax him, take him outside of himself as he concentrated on the task at hand. Today was not one of those days. For the life of him he couldn't shake seeing Desiree with Max DeLaine, of all people. He'd always imagined her as being above all of that. Well, not above it, but rather not of it. Status and standing had never appeared to be a pursuit of Desiree's. At least he hadn't thought so. That had always been Dominique's thing. Name and recognition. Apparently he was wrong.

The hissing coming from behind him drew his attention. He turned to find his pot of crawfish bubbling over, the brew spewing onto the stove top, which was most unfortunate since it was a crucial part of the dipping sauce.

"Damn it!" Without thinking, he snatched off the cover and the scalding metal singed his fingertips, sending the pot cover sliding and clanging across the black-and-white tiled kitchen floor.

"You okay, chef?" one of his cooks asked, hurrying to his side. He picked up the pot cover and dropped it in the industrial sink.

Spence was shaking his mildly injured hand and wiping up the stove-top mess with the other. "I'm good. Thanks." He shooed him away and turned back to assess his handiwork. Thankfully it wasn't as bad as it appeared. More messy than anything else, and he still had plenty of the juice left for the dip.

That was totally unlike him, he thought as he began dicing scallions and chili peppers. Care in the kitchen was always a mandate for him and his entire staff. It was much too easy to have a major accident when you weren't paying attention. He drained the pot, catching most of the juice in another huge pot and leaving just enough to cover the crawfish. He poured the spices, scallions and peppers into the juice and turned the flame on low for ten minutes before pouring the crawfish back into the seasoned broth. He set the timer, then went to check on the other cooking stations: meat, fish, dessert.

Satisfied, he hung up his apron and went out front to check in with the reservations hostess, Nichole.

Spence knocked on the closed door.

"Come in."

Spence stuck his head in. "Busy?"

"Hi, Spence," Nichole greeted, her sunshine smile in sharp contrast to the tight, cramped space that she worked out of. But it didn't seem to phase her one bit. Spence had promised her that as soon as they could expand, he would get her an office that was worthy of her. Nichole had been with him almost since he'd opened. She was in her late twenties, single, smart and was a dead ringer for the supermodel Naomi Campbell. Not as tall but equally as lovely and definitely not as feisty. Nichole was about as calm and easygoing as they came. And no matter how irate a customer became or how crazy an evening turned out to be when the restaurant bubbled over in terms of capacity, she never lost her cool or her charm. And she always got a kick out of the quick second looks she would receive when people thought she was Naomi Campbell.

"Hey, Nikki. Just wanted to check on what things were looking like for tonight."

She turned to her computer screen and pulled up the reservation list. "All of the reservations except for three have been confirmed. So that's sixty-five reservations for a total of one hundred thirty people. We have room for another seventy walk-ins. And of course we stop seating at nine." She looked up at him and grinned.

"Another busy night."

"Looks that way."

"How're you doing in school?"

She leaned back just a bit in her seat. "Pretty good. One more semester and I'm done." She paused a moment, tugged on her bottom lip with her teeth. "Um, I know you're pretty close with the Lawson family...."

His pulse jumped. "Yeah, I've known them for a while. What's up?"

Nichole lowered her head, shoved some papers around for a moment. "I was wondering how well you knew Justin Lawson." She licked her lips.

"Oh." Spence's sleek brows rose and fell. "Hmm, not as well as the rest of the family. He was much younger when I first met them all and then he was in school. Didn't really see him much." His brow wrinkled. He tipped his head slightly to the side. "Both of you are at LSU, right?"

Nichole nodded.

Spence leaned against the jamb of the door, afraid to move his solid frame around the small space and knock down her perfect stacks of folders and files.

"He seems like a nice guy," Nichole said.

Spence waited for something more.

She drew in a breath and picked up her pen, twirled it between her fingers.

"Well, I better get back to the kitchen. Thanks for the update," he said.

"Sure, anytime."

He turned to leave, then turned back. "I get the feeling that you want to ask me something. You can, you know."

Her dark brown eyes moved swiftly across his face. She swallowed. "I was just wondering if…maybe sometime you could formally introduce us." All her facial features pinched, as if her body was in pain.

The corner of Spence's full mouth curved upward. "Sure." He shrugged his right shoulder. "Not a problem."

She waved her hand. "No, no. Forget I said anything. That was so awkward and unprofessional." She covered her face with her hands and groaned.

Spence dared to ease into the room. He stood in front of her desk. "Hey, don't stress yourself. I can't guarantee anything, but I can see that you get to meet him."

"Thanks," she murmured.

He winked. "Not a problem." He turned and left, chuckling to himself. Justin was a good guy and he knew Nichole was a great young woman. He'd do what he could and leave the rest up to fate.

He was thinking about Nichole's request and studying his shoes as he walked down the narrow hall just as Michelle stepped out of her office, and he ran right into her.

"Sorry." He clasped her shoulders. "You okay?"

She bobbed her head. "Yeah, fine." She gazed up at him and felt her heart hammering in her chest. His fingertips heated her skin. There had been too many nights, especially recently, when she sorely regretted ending their affair. Logic dictated that it was best to totally separate business from pleasure, and since neither of them wanted strings, there was no headache. But it took not being with him—that way—to make her realize what a mistake she'd made in cutting the invisible strings. Each day it got harder. She'd even thought about quitting, but then she probably wouldn't see him at all. "Where are you in such a hurry to go?"

"Back to the kitchen. I was checking with Nikki. Looks like another full house."

"I told you I intended to turn this into Baton Rouge's number one hot spot. By the way, don't forget to tie down Rafe. I'd love to get him booked sooner rather than later."

"I'll give him a call. This time he promised me. Have to firm up a date."

"Great." She drew in a breath. "Um, I was wondering... If you're not busy next Sunday...I thought maybe we could do something."

His mouth flickered. "Uh...do something?"

She swallowed, focused on the cleft in his chin and not on the searchlights that peered into her soul. She shrugged and shifted her weight. "Movie...brunch..." She tucked her sleek auburn hair behind her ear.

"Michelle...I don't know if that's a good idea. I mean—"

She held up her hand and forced herself to smile when she really felt like crawling into a hole. "Listen, forget it. Just a passing thought. We haven't hung out together in...forever to just talk and catch up. I was just thinking... Forget it." She sputtered a nervous laugh.

He reached for her just as Nichole came out of her office.

"Hey, guys," Nichole chirped and squeezed by them.

"I need to check the stockroom," Michelle said, excused herself, stepped around him and walked in the opposite direction.

Spence watched her until she turned the corner.

He shook his head, a little unsettled by what had just transpired. It had been years since there had been anything beyond business between him and Michelle. They'd both decided that they wanted it that way. And as far as he knew, it was working.

But when he'd looked at her just now, what he saw in her eyes and felt in the heat that radiated off her body was not the emotions of a platonic business associate, but those of a warm flesh-and-blood woman who wanted more than a handshake and a kiss on the cheek.

Maybe it was a bad move on his part to have taken Michelle to the dinner party last night. Maybe that gave her the idea that something was happening that actually wasn't.

Spence returned to the kitchen. They'd have to talk. He didn't want there to be any bruised feelings or to create an uncomfortable work environment. Michelle was like his right hand and he didn't want to jeopardize that, but more important he didn't want to fracture their friendship. He exhaled a breath of mild frustration. *Women. Gotta love them.*

"You have a date!" Patrice squeaked as she pierced the meat of the mussel with her fork and lifted it to her mouth. "And with Maxwell DeLaine. Girl…still waters run deep."

"Damn, Trice, you don't have to act like it's the discovery of eternal life or something."

Patrice pointed her fork at Desiree. "It is just as amazing. For real."

Desiree huffed. Was she really that hopeless that

something as simple as a date was almost newsworthy? That didn't do much for her ego. It had been months since she'd been out with a man for an occasion that wasn't business related. But she'd been busy, she consoled herself. She pushed her shrimp salad around on her plate.

"Did he say where he's taking you?"

"No. He said he would make the reservations."

Patrice watched her friend. "And you don't want to go, is that it?"

Desiree glanced up. "It's not that." Her gaze darted around the restaurant, taking in the lunchtime crowd, then settled back on Patrice's face.

"Okay, so what is it, then? 'Cause you sure don't look like a woman who is on the verge of going out with one of the most eligible bachelors in the state of Louisiana."

Desiree drew in a long breath. She put down her fork, pushed her plate aside and folded her arms across the table. "There's something I want to tell you...well, talk to you about."

Patrice stopped chewing. Her expression shifted to mirror the seriousness that had settled around them. "Sure. What is it?"

"It's about Spence Hampton."

Patrice frowned. "What about him?"

"The reason why I'm not interested in other men is because of Spence."

Patrice blinked in confusion. "Wait, I don't understand. You've been seeing Spence?"

Desiree shook her head. "No. I haven't been seeing

him…but I want to. I've wanted to for quite some time."

"Let me get this straight. You have a thing for Spence Hampton. He's the reason why you don't date or keep a relationship going for more than a hot minute. And apparently he knows nothing about it…like *I* didn't." She lifted her glass of sweet tea and brought it to her pouting lips.

Desiree flinched from the sting of Patrice's tone. She jerked her head back. "You're *pissed* because I didn't tell you?" she asked, her voice rising with incredulity.

Patrice leaned forward. "We're best friends. I tell you everything. I mean, come on, Desi. Here I am, making a fool of myself trying to hook you up with this one and that one and you already have your mind made up. Why didn't you just say something?"

"I'm not going to apologize for not telling you. It's something I've been battling with for a lot of reasons."

"Like what?"

Desiree paused for a long moment, trying to think how to frame what she was about to say. Finally she simply blurted it out. "Like I think Spence and Dom have had a thing…you know. And I just couldn't…"

Patrice's expression softened. "Wow. I guess from the outside looking in, you would get that impression. To be truthful, I thought the same thing."

"See!"

"Have you asked her?"

"Absolutely not."

"Why?"

"Because it's not my business who my sister sleeps with."

"Could it also be that you really don't want to know, because if you did, you'd finally have to make a decision about him?"

Desiree glanced away from the truth, then met it head-on. "Yes," she quietly confessed.

"Limbo is a lousy place to be, sis."

"Don't I know it."

"What are you going to do?"

Desiree leaned back against the leather seating. "Go out with Max DeLaine. Start dating again. Explore some options and get Spence out of my head once and for all."

"You're going to go along with Dom's crazy match-making marathon?"

Desiree chuckled. "If there is one thing I do know for sure about my sister, it is that when she makes up her mind to get something done, it's done. I've given her two months." She jabbed at a shrimp.

"And that's another thing," Patrice complained. "How many times have I tried to get you to double-date? Turned me down flat. Always had an excuse. I thought I was—"

"Okay, okay, I'm sorry. Forgive me for my transgressions," Desiree said to cut her off before she got really wound up. "I promise I'll tell you everything from now on. I'll even go out on a double date."

Patrice's light brown eyes widened. "You will, for real?"

"Yes, I will."

Patrice leaned back, momentarily placated. "Good. So see how this goes with Max, and maybe if you feel comfortable, we can set up something in a couple of weeks."

Desiree bobbed her head. "Okay." She checked her watch. "I have to get back to the office." She took out her wallet from her purse.

"Don't worry about it. I'll get the check. Go on back. I'm going to relax a bit and take in the scenery," she said, eyeing a young, strapping brother that had just walked in, in what appeared to be a very expensive suit.

Desiree followed Patrice's gaze and shook her head. She pushed back from her seat and stood. "Next one is on me."

"Let me know how the date goes."

"You'll be the first one I call."

"I'm holding you to that."

Desiree finger waved and walked out.

Patrice watched her leave and wondered if Desiree really could get Spence Hampton out of her system and if *she* could somehow find out if Spence and Dominique had been more than just friends.

Chapter 8

Desiree pulled her black Volvo into the private outdoor parking lot for Mansurs on Corporate Boulevard. Traffic at this time of the evening was always brutal and she was supremely thankful for the small amenity of private parking. It saved her from circling the neighborhood.

She pulled her car up to the booth, got out and took her ticket from the agent, then walked around to the front entrance. The instant she opened the door, the mouthwatering aroma of the Creole cuisine that Mansurs was known for welcomed her with open arms. She stepped into the dimly lit confines of the restaurant and approached the concierge's table.

"Good evening, ma'am. Do you have a reservation?" asked the young woman, who didn't look old enough to drive.

"Good evening. I'm meeting someone. The reservation will be in their name. Maxwell DeLaine."

Her brows rose. "Oh, Mr. DeLaine." She practically bubbled over. "He's here. I'll be happy to take you to his table." She gathered up a menu. "Please, follow me. I'll take you right to him. He hasn't been waiting long, but he wanted to make sure you were seated as soon as you arrived."

Desiree didn't know whether to be impressed or a bit frightened at the level of enthusiasm. She followed the young woman to the back of the restaurant, where she was shown a banquette, separated from the rest of the restaurant by beveled glass.

"Mr. DeLaine, your guest has arrived." She gingerly placed a menu on the table, as if it had suddenly turned to fine china.

Maxwell stood. "Thank you, Kim." The young woman beamed and hurried away. Maxwell focused on Desiree. A warm smile put a sparkle in his eyes. He came around the table and politely kissed her cheek before helping her into her seat.

Desiree settled herself. "I get the impression that you and Kim know each other."

He chuckled lightly. "She was a former student of mine. I know the guy that owns the restaurant and she needed a job." He shrugged off the rest of his comment. "Would you like a drink?"

She drew in a breath. "Yes, I would." She thanked him with a smile and wondered once again if she had pegged him wrong. She was going to make it a point to put his family name aside and give him a chance. Of all people, she should know the weight that a family name could carry—both good and bad. "Apple martini."

Max signaled for the waiter. "The lady will have an apple martini."

"Can I freshen your bourbon, sir?"

"Yes, thanks." He turned to Desiree. "You look wonderful."

She lowered her gaze. "Thank you." She reached for her glass of water to give her hands something to do.

"I hear there is a rezoning forum coming up. You're involved with that."

"Yes. The parish has been very vocal in their displeasure. It's been a residential community for decades and the rezoning would allow for a shopping mall and businesses to open within that community."

The waiter returned with their drinks.

Max lifted his glass and touched Desiree's.

"Obviously, the rezoning will bring in much-needed jobs," Max said.

"Of course, but at the expense of a certain quality of life." She sighed. "So that's the battle."

"Not easy."

She sipped her drink.

"How is it?"

"Perfect." She smiled and set her glass down.

The waitress approached. "Are you ready to order?"

"Ready?" Max looked to Desiree.

"Yes. I'll have the blackened salmon with saffron rice and the house salad."

"And you, sir?"

"Make that two."

The waitress took the menus. "It will be about twenty minutes. Would you like an appetizer before then?"

Desiree declined.

"Nothing for me, either." He cupped his drink. "I've been keeping up with the election campaigns. Looks like your father will secure another term."

Desiree grinned. "My dad is determined that they will take him kicking and screaming out of office."

"And now you have a brother-in-law in politics, as well. Seems like it definitely runs in the family. Have you ever considered running for office?"

"Actually, I have. I wanted to get a few good years of local politics under my belt first so that I have a platform and support from my constituents."

He nodded. "The Lawson name carries a lot of weight. I'm sure you'll get the support you need." He sipped his drink.

"Is that what you think? That I'll get by on my name?"

Max set his drink down. "It can't hurt."

"Is that how you got your position at Southern University? By using the DeLaine name?"

The corner of his mouth lifted. "In this world in order to get ahead, you sometimes have to use every advantage that is available to you. Would I have gotten the position without it?" He shrugged his right shoulder. "Probably. But the cachet of DeLaine and everything that it represents eased the journey."

Desiree leaned back in her seat and took him in. As much as she'd wanted to give him the benefit of the doubt, that notion was just nixed. "I see."

The waitress returned with their meal and set the plates in front of them. "Can I get you anything else?" she asked, looking from one to the other.

They both chorused no.

Max cut into his salmon. "I get the feeling that what I said doesn't sit well with you. Tell me why."

"All my life I've been saddled with the legacy of Lawson. Because of that a lot is expected of us. And not because of who we are as individuals, but because of what we represent. I don't want to get what I want because of who my father is, or my brother-in-law or my other siblings. I want it because I deserve it and I worked for it and earned it."

He chewed thoughtfully. "Do you think I simply gained a professorship without the credentials to back it up?"

"That's the way you make it sound."

He put down his fork and wiped his lips with the white linen napkin. Desiree took a sip of her drink to steady her nerves. He was really beginning to piss her off.

"I have two master's degrees, one in art history and one in ancient languages, and I recently finished my doctorate in world history. When I applied for the position at Southern, did my family name get me in? Of course. Having a DeLaine on the staff provides extra value to the university. But it wouldn't have gotten me very far if I didn't have the credentials to back up my name." He released a long breath. "If I'd wanted to take the easy route in life, I could have joined one of my father's many firms and been installed as CEO without having to get out of bed. But who my father is and what he does are not who I am or what I want." He paused. "Much like you." His expression softened. An inviting smile graced his mouth.

Desiree lowered her gaze. Why was she so eager to paint him into a corner? She looked across at him and stretched out her hand. "I'm Desiree."

He took her hand in his. "Maxwell. But all my friends call me Max."

She breathed a little easier. "Did I mention that I love art but can't tell one period piece from the other?"

He chuckled. "I'd be more than happy to share my vast wealth of knowledge with you. Most women I date can't seem to appreciate the finer things in life."

Inwardly she flinched. "Meaning?"

He reached across the table and gently covered her hand with his. "Meaning you're not like those other women—and you're the one I'm with. Their loss."

Desiree slowly eased her hand away. "So…um tell me about some of your favorite paintings…"

"I hope tonight won't be the last." Maxwell opened her car door. "My offer for an art gallery tour is still open."

Desiree faced him and gave a faint smile.

"I'll call you." He hesitated a beat before gently clasping her shoulders and kissing her fully on her lips.

Desiree gasped in surprise, not sure if she was simply stunned or offended, but before she could react he took a step back, opened her car door and she quickly slid in behind the wheel.

"Drive safe."

She fastened her seat belt. "You, too."

Max shut her door and moved aside as she pulled out of her spot. He stuck his hand in the pocket of his slacks and strode off toward his vehicle. He had every intention of seeing Desiree Lawson again. She was the kind of woman he'd been looking for.

Spence stood across the street from Mansurs, watching the scene unfold. As was his habit on Tuesday nights, he randomly stopped into some of the top and up-and-coming restaurants to see what his competition was doing. The last two people he expected to see together were Desiree and Maxwell DeLaine. Obviously they'd hit it off.

He crossed the street and went inside.

"Do you have a reservation, sir?" the hostess asked.

"No. I'll sit at the bar."

"Certainly."

He approached the bar and sat down.

The bartender placed a bowl of nuts and pretzels in front of him. "What can I get you?"

"Double scotch. No ice." He needed something strong to mute what he'd seen and loosen the knot in his gut. He needed to move on, he thought, taking the first hot shot of his drink. The cinnamon-colored liquid burst with heat and flavor on the way down. And his moving on would begin tonight. It had been a while since he'd contacted Melanie Harte's exclusive dating service. In the past she'd connected him with some great women. The problem had never been with them, but with his subconscious comparing them to Desiree. None of them ever quite made the grade.

He took another long swallow of his drink and set the tumbler down, closing his eyes against the fire that reignited in his belly, then shot to his head. First thing tomorrow he'd give Melanie a call and see if she could work her magic.

Spence signaled for the bartender. "I'll have another double."

Chapter 9

Spence awoke to the smell of fresh-brewed coffee and his dog Howard licking his arm. He slowly sat up and the jackhammers went off in his head. "Hey, boy," he muttered. He pressed his hand against his forehead and shut his eyes against the glare of the morning sun. He drew in slow, deep breaths to try to clear his head and that was when he heard noise coming from his kitchen. But that was impossible. He lived alone.

With a lot of concentration he put his feet on the floor and stood up. The room shifted, then settled. He crossed the room and saw a pair of women's heels next to his armoire and a black skirt and blouse casually tossed across the chair. He frowned. What the hell...

He pulled open his bedroom door and crossed the hall and went out into the small living room that opened onto the kitchen and there was Michelle, in one of his dress shirts, standing at his stove. He shook his head to dispel the hallucination but she was still there.

"Michelle?"

She turned from scrambling eggs in the frying pan. "Hey, you're up. How's your head?"

He stepped farther into the room and realized he had on only his boxers. "What are you doing here?"

She switched off the flame and turned fully toward him. Only two buttons were fastened and he could tell that all she had on beneath his shirt was a tiny pair of red panties. He glanced away and sat down at the island counter. He couldn't get his brain to work fast enough to process what was going on and his imagination painted the worst.

"I guess you don't remember calling me from Mansurs at 2:00 a.m.?" She poured a cup of coffee and handed it to him.

His head pounded. He tried to think. The previous night came in and out in flashes. He remembered seeing Desiree and Maxwell. He frowned, forcing the images to come together and make sense. He saw himself sitting at the bar and ordering doubles. He glanced across at Michelle. He remembered trying to call his buddy Dexter to come and pick him up and not getting an answer.

The pieces began falling into place. The bartender insisted that he not leave until someone came to get him. He'd called Michelle. She came and drove him home. After that it was all a blank. He silently prayed that it was because he'd come home and passed out.

"Drink your coffee. You'll feel better." She hopped up onto a stool opposite him.

Spence took a sip of the piping hot coffee and looked at Michelle over the rim of the mug. Nothing clicked.

"Feel like eating something?"

He blinked her back into focus. "Naw. Thanks. Coffee is fine." He stood. "I'm gonna go take a shower." He took the mug with him and headed to the bathroom.

Under the beat of the shower and with the aromatic scent of his favorite soap, he felt the fog begin to clear. She'd brought him home and he'd stumbled into his bedroom. She'd helped him out of his clothes and he'd tumbled into bed. End of story. Nothing had happened between them, and in the condition that he'd come home in, even if it had, it wouldn't have been much fun for either of them.

He held his face up to the spray. The last time he drank like that was back in college, when he was young and stupid. Apparently he'd regressed. At least he didn't get behind the wheel and he didn't sleep with Michelle. He turned off the water and stepped out of the stall, grabbed a towel and mopped his face before wrapping it around his waist. His stomach jerked. Where did she sleep last night?

Spence stepped out of the bathroom into his adjoining bedroom and stopped cold in his tracks. Michelle was in the center of his bedroom, in front of his dresser mirror, brushing her hair with nothing on but a bra and thong that left more to the imagination than it covered.

She turned at the sound of his entry, her hands raised above her head as she pulled her hair into a ponytail.

The simple gesture enhanced her finely tuned body. He'd almost forgotten how incredible she looked beneath her clothing. She was an avid pilates enthusiast and it showed.

"I was waiting for you to come out so that I could take a quick shower." She lowered her arms and stood provocatively in front of him. "I hope you don't mind."

He tried to pull his gaze away but she made it extremely difficult.

"Feeling better?" Her eyes moved slowly over him, then returned to his face.

He could feel her body heat radiating off of her. He took a step around her. "Yeah. Much."

She grabbed his bare shoulder. He turned his head in her direction, and before he could react, she kissed him. Her full breast grazed his arm. Her soft moan was like a song in his ears. She pressed her body against his and he felt the quick tightening in his groin. Her arm snaked around his neck and with her free hand she tugged at the towel wrapped around his waist.

"Touch me," she whispered against his lips. She took his hand and covered her breast with it.

He felt the tremor that rippled through her. Instinct and long-abated need rushed to the surface. His towel dropped to the floor, revealing his erection, which was rock hard and pulsing.

Michelle took him in her palm and stroked him in a slow up-and-down rhythm that turned the muscles of his thighs into throbbing ropes.

His body wanted her. Wanted the release, the pleasure that being within her would give him. Memories of the hot, lusty sexcapades between them played in his head, intensified with her touch.

Spence grabbed her wrist to stop what another stroke would urge to the surface. "Chell…" He pulled away.

Michelle staggered. Her chest heaved as if she'd been running. She leaned against the wall. "Wh-what? What's wrong?"

Spence picked up the towel from the floor and tied it back around his waist. "We're not going to do this."

She blinked in disbelief. She started toward him. He held up his hand.

"No, Michelle. It's been over between us for a long time. It's what we both decided."

Her bottom lip trembled. "What if I changed my mind?" Her voice shook.

Spence lowered his head and tried to find the right words that wouldn't do more damage than had already been done.

"Michelle." He leaned against the dresser. "It can't work. We both know that."

"Why? Because I'm not *her?*"

His head jerked back. "What? You're not who?"

Suddenly she felt naked. She pressed her lips together, grabbed her clothes from the chair and walked to the bathroom. "You're right," she said from over her shoulder. "It can't work." She shut the door behind her.

Spence grabbed some boxers from his dresser drawer, tugged on some jeans and pulled a body-hugging white T-shirt over his head. He listened to the shower water running. How the hell did they get here? He paced the room, scrubbing his face with his hand, before walking out into the kitchen. He poured a fresh cup of coffee and sat down at the counter.

Shortly after, Michelle appeared in the doorway of the kitchen. Spence jumped up.

"Michelle…"

"Don't. It's okay. I totally understand and you're right." She forced a tight smile and lowered her gaze. "I'm thinking I'll take today off." She glanced at him, then turned and walked out.

Spence blew out a ragged breath and slumped back onto his seat. How could he have let something like this happen? He jumped up, darted down the hall, grabbed his jacket and keys and went after her. He couldn't leave things like this between them. Michelle didn't deserve that. He ran outside just in time to see Michelle's Lexus turn the corner.

He trotted to a halt and stood in the center of the street, with the growing sense that this mess he'd gotten himself into would get worse before it got better. And what did Michelle mean by "her"?

Chapter 10

Desiree returned to her desk after her second meeting of the day and it was only 11:00 a.m. The light on her phone blinked with the messages that waited for her. She picked up the handset and went through all ten of them, three of which were from her sister Dominique, wanting to know how her date with Max went. She made a note of the other calls that she had to return.

How *did* the date with Max go? She hadn't had much time to think about it. On a scale of one to ten she would rate it a six. Max was a decent guy. Smart, ambitious, handsome, sure of himself, too sure of himself judging by the kiss and that statement about other women. Maybe she should have been flattered but she wasn't. On the surface, he had it all, including an endless bank account and all the right connections. He could easily make a woman very happy. Unfortunately, she didn't think that woman was her.

She wanted to feel something, some spark, some magic, some thrill when she thought about Max. It simply wasn't there. There was no overwhelming desire to see him again or anticipation of his next phone call, which was what she had told her disbelieving sister that evening over dinner.

"You have got to be kidding me. You don't like him?"

"I didn't say that I didn't like him. I said I wasn't interested in taking it any further."

Dominique lifted her glass of wine and took a small sip. "I don't understand it. Women are standing in line, waiting on a chance with Maxwell DeLaine."

"I'm not one of them." She got up from the table and put her dish in the dishwasher. She turned to face her sister. "Sorry."

"So are you going with him to the museum?"

"I don't think that'll be a good idea. I don't want to lead him on. I was planning on calling him this evening before he called me."

Dominique folded her arms. "I hope you won't regret this later."

"I doubt it."

Dominique pushed back from the table. "We still have forty days left to our agreement." She opened the dishwasher and put in her plate and utensils.

Desiree heaved a sigh. "Yes, and they can't be over soon enough for me."

"That's not the attitude to take. You should be looking

forward to this as much as I am." She smiled broadly and wagged a finger at her sister. "I'm gonna find the right man for you if I have to hunt down every eligible man in the state of Louisiana." She sashayed away.

Desiree groaned, turned on the dishwasher and went to her room. She stretched out across her bed and suddenly had the overwhelming need to talk with her big sister. She checked the time. It was a little after eight. Hopefully Lee Ann was settled in and her call wouldn't disturb Lee Ann and Preston's time together.

She reached for the phone and dialed Lee Ann's number in D.C. Lee Ann answered on the third ring.

"Desi, how are you? This is a treat."

Desiree could hear the smile in her big sister's voice. "Hey, sis. Hope I didn't catch you at a bad time."

"Not at all. I was actually lounging." She laughed. "Preston had a late meeting and hasn't gotten in yet. So I'm taking some time for me. What's going on? How are things at the homestead?"

"Pretty good. Everyone here is fine."

"Hmm, umm, I hear a *but* in there somewhere. What's going on?"

Desiree rested against her stack of pillows and crossed her feet. "Well…I sort of made this deal with Dominique…."

When she finished telling her sister about it, she held her breath, wondering what Lee Ann would say.

"Dom never changes," Lee Ann said, with a sprinkle of humor in her voice. "She could talk a poor man out of his last quarter. My advice, if you want my advice, is to be up front with her. Tell her you've thought about it and this 'deal' is not what you want. Or you can suck it up for the next forty days. Make the most of it, have some fun and, who knows, you might find someone that you actually like."

"I guess," she said on a sigh.

"Are you sure that's all that's bothering you?"

She so wanted to tell her sister about Spence, her feelings for him and her suspicions about his relationship with Dominique. But she couldn't. It wouldn't be fair to Lee Ann to get her in the middle of that, especially if she might know anything about Dominique and Spence.

"Yeah, that's it. Dom can be a bit relentless when she puts her mind on something."

"Don't I know it? Remember that time when she wanted a dog…?"

They laughed and talked for a few more minutes, until Desiree heard Preston greeting his wife in the background.

"I'll let you go," Desiree said. "Tell Preston hello for me."

"I sure will. And don't let Dom sweet-talk you into doing something you don't want to do."

"I won't. Thanks, sis. Love you."

"Love you, too."

She disconnected the call and returned the receiver to the base. Maybe Lee Ann was right. She should just relax and try to have some fun. Maybe she would find someone. She just hated feeling like a charity case, though, or another one of her sister's experiments. She flipped onto her side and turned out the bedside lamp. At least she had something to look forward to. This weekend she would be out on the track and could put all this dating business on the back burner.

The last of the dinner customers were gone and Nichole, who'd filled in for Michelle, locked up behind them. She couldn't remember Michelle being out on a day that was not her usual day off. If anything, Michelle was wedded to her job and gave the impression to the staff that she was needed at every juncture. Tonight Nichole could at least prove that wasn't true. She'd run the restaurant with as much expertise and finesse as Michelle had ever done. She felt confident that Spence would feel the same way.

"Everything is shut tight," Nichole said as she stepped up next to Spence, who was closing down the kitchen.

He glanced at her over his shoulder. "Thanks."

"The night receipts are ready for deposit. I can put them in the drop box on my way home."

"Sure." He turned off the overhead lights above the grills.

"Um, will Michelle be coming in tomorrow?"

"I don't know." He walked toward the swinging doors where Nichole stood.

"Is everything okay?"

Spence finally looked at her. He forced a smile. "Yeah."

"You seem distracted."

He took his jacket from a hook behind the door. "Lots on my mind."

She nodded and wished that he would say something

about the job she'd done. It was the first time she had to handle the running of the restaurant on her own.

He pushed one of the doors open and let her pass. He switched off the lights and walked out behind her.

"Um, if you need me to take care of things tomorrow, I'd be more than happy to do it."

"Sure," he murmured. "I'll let you know."

Spence unlocked the front door and set the alarm. They walked out together. He accompanied Nichole to her car.

"Well, good night," she said quietly.

"Hey…listen, thanks for tonight. I appreciate it."

"No problem." She paused a beat. "Are you sure you're okay?"

He focused on her, took in the look of concern in her eyes. He put a hand on her shoulder. "I'm fine, really. You get home safely. I'll see you tomorrow."

She nodded and opened the door of her car and got in. He waited until she had buckled up and pulled away before walking to his car.

The truth was, he wasn't all right. Michelle's absence was his fault. He'd tried to contact her all day with no results. He'd left several messages and she had not returned his calls. He was at a loss as to what to do. All he could hope for was that she turned up tomorrow or at least returned his calls. He had to make this right.

Chapter 11

Desiree had attempted several times to reach Max, but each time she'd gone for the phone, some other crisis in the office had pulled her away. Now the day was over and Valerie told her that there was a very handsome gentleman waiting to see her in the reception area.

Desiree frowned. "Who is it? I don't have any appointments scheduled."

Valerie grinned like she'd won the lotto. "Max DeLaine. Is he who I think he is?"

Desiree's stomach tightened. She pushed back from her desk. "Depends on who you think he is," she said, trying to make light of it.

"One of the most eligible bachelors in the state, for starters."

"So I've heard." She walked around her desk to her

office door and out front, passing several cubicles, with Valerie trailing behind her.

Max was seated in one of the tan plastic chairs, flipping through a magazine. He glanced up at her approach, stood and greeted her with his devastating smile. For a moment she felt bad about what she was on the brink of saying.

"Max, I wasn't expecting you." She stepped up to him.

He leaned down, took the hand that she extended and lightly kissed her cheek. "I know I should have called first, but I was hoping I could talk you into having dinner with me tonight."

"Oh...I..." She eased her hand from his.

"It is spur of the moment and I should have realized that you already had plans."

"No, it's not that. I'd planned to call you last night and then today."

He took a step back—waited.

Desiree released a breath, took a quick glance around. "Max, you're wonderful. I had a great time with you, but...I don't think it will work and I don't want to lead you on." She clasped her hands together as she watched his lips flicker ever so slightly.

He shifted his weight. "I'd hoped for a different response, but I appreciate your honesty." He drew himself up. "The offer for the tour is always open. Take care."

Desiree watched him walk out and felt utterly horrible. Hurting people's feelings no matter how slight was something she worked to avoid at all costs. *Better now than later,* she consoled herself and headed back to her office, but not before being waylaid by Valerie.

"Well…what happened? What did he want? Are you seeing him?"

"No, I'm not seeing him." She opened her office door. "And please, no more questions about Max DeLaine."

Valerie flinched. "Fine," she murmured.

Desiree turned to face Valerie. "Sorry. I didn't mean to snap. It's not you. Really. It's complicated and personal. I'd just rather not talk about it."

As much as Desiree admired and respected Valerie, she was, after all, her employee. And she was not in the habit of sharing her personal life in general, but especially not with employees in particular.

"I understand. I was a little starstuck." She leaned against the door frame, folded her arms.

Desiree took some files from the cabinet. "He is a good-looking man," she said off-handedly.

"I wouldn't kick him out of bed."

"Good to know," Desiree said. She rounded her desk and sat down, folded her hands on top of a short stack of folders.

Valerie checked her watch. "I'm going to head on out, unless you need anything."

"No. Go home. Craig and Lizzie still here?"

"Lizzie is. Craig left about an hour ago. How much longer are you planning to stay?"

"Maybe another fifteen minutes. I want to review the last set of details on the rezoning."

"I'll see you in the morning."

"Night."

Alone now, Desiree had the chance to gather her thoughts about Maxwell. It was the best thing. She wasn't "feeling him," as the kids would say. He would eventually find someone that he could be happy with, and she knew that someone wasn't her. She shut off her computer, put the folders back in the file cabinet, grabbed her things and headed out. She stopped at Lizzie's cubicle to say good-night and found that she was already gone.

Desiree turned off the lights and stepped outside. Twilight had settled over the city, that in-between time of day and night that gave the world an almost dreamlike quality. Nothing was as it seemed. She locked the front door and started down the street to her car. She was halfway down the block when the door of a black Lincoln suddenly opened and Max stepped out in front of her.

Desiree drew in a sharp breath of alarm. She gripped her cell phone. "Max." She sputtered a nervous laugh. "You scared me. What are you still doing here?" Her heart pounded.

"Thought I'd wait around and maybe you would change your mind."

"What?" She was getting a very bad feeling. "I haven't changed my mind." She glanced at her phone, ready to dial 911.

"Rejection is not good for the ego. I thought you were different from those other women." He reached out to touch her and she drew back. He held up his hand. "I'm sorry. Look, I know this seems crazy, like something on television. I just wanted to talk."

"I've got to go. My brother is expecting me." It was the first thing that came to her head. She stepped around him.

"Desiree, I only want to talk, that's all," he called out as she hurried down the street.

Her pulse was hammering in her ears. She wanted to run. Every few feet she looked over her shoulder, expecting him to suddenly be right behind her.

Her hands shook as she chirped the alarm and ducked into her car. She immediately locked the door and turned the car on. Her phone rang and she nearly leaped out of her seat. She grabbed the phone. It was Patrice.

"Patrice!"

"What's wrong?"

Desiree started talking so fast, Patrice had to tell her to slow down.

"Max…he showed up at my office and then he was… waiting for me…."

"Where are you right this second?"

"In my car."

"Meet me at Bottoms Up or I'm coming there for you."

She turned on her headlights. "I'm on my way."

"And, Desi…"

"Yeah?"

"Just hurry."

It was a fifteen-minute drive. Desiree was there in ten, her heart racing the entire time. She pulled up in front of Bottoms Up and Patrice was right outside. She ran over to Desiree's car.

Desiree unlocked the door and Patrice jumped in.

"Are you okay?" Her gaze ran over Desiree like a surgeon's. "Did he touch you? What the hell happened?"

Desiree drew in several long breaths. "It was odd and scary. It was nothing that he said, just the look on his face and in his eyes. The whole idea that he would wait for me…" She gave a little shiver.

"I say we report it. You can't take any chances these days. Just because he's rich doesn't mean he ain't crazy."

Desiree covered Patrice's hand with her own. "I don't think that's necessary."

"Desi…"

"No. I'm okay. He didn't do anything. And what am I going to report? That he was waiting for me after work to ask if we could talk? They'd laugh me out of the station."

"Hell, no, they won't. You're Senator Lawson's daughter."

"Exactly. The last thing I need or want is reporters swooping in on me. Which is exactly what they would do. They can smell a story a mile away." She shook her head and held up her hand. "No, thank you."

"I don't agree, but if that's what you want."

They sat in tense silence.

"If you'd just told Spence how you feel, none of this would have happened."

Desiree snapped her head toward Patrice and the fact that she was sitting in front of Spence's restaurant finally sank in.

"What are you doing here, anyway? Did you say something to him? Patrice, I swear…"

"No! I didn't say anything. I stopped in—" she shrugged a little "—to have an after-work drink and maybe…see Spence." She tried to shrink into the seat.

"Trice! This is the exact reason why I didn't say anything to you in the first place. I'm going home." She turned the car on.

Patrice clasped her arm. "Aw, come on. I didn't say anything. And I'm not letting you go home by yourself."

Desiree jerked her neck back. "What are you going to do? Follow me home? Don't be crazy."

"What if he's waiting for you at the house?"

"I doubt it." But the idea made her insides tighten. "I'll call Rafe."

"Rafe is inside."

"Huh?"

"He's inside. He's sitting in on one of the sets."

"He didn't say anything about playing here tonight."

"Nothing official. He stopped in and Spence asked if he wanted to play. That was the reason for my call."

Desiree turned off the car. "Come on."

They went inside and found Rafe at the bar, chatting it up with a female bartender.

"Hey, big brother." She came up and hugged him from behind.

Rafe slowly swung around on the stool. "Desi." He was all smiles and charm. He curled his arm around her waist. "What brings you here tonight, Cher?"

"Patrice called and told me you were going to be playing."

"Just sitting in on a set. See how it feels. Can I get you ladies a drink?"

"Apple martini for me," Patrice said.

"A white wine."

Rafe placed their orders just as Spence approached.

"Desiree…this is a surprise." He kissed her cheek, wanted to linger there but pulled away.

"Good to see you, Spence." Her heart fluttered.

"How've you been?"

For an instant she was caught up in the embrace of his gaze. "Good," she finally said. "I see you managed to get my brother down here."

Spence chuckled. "Yeah, a major coup," he joked. "Staying for dinner?"

"I'm not sure."

"Well, whatever you want is on the house." He stared a moment too long, then turned to Rafe. "The band will be ready for you in a few. You want to come on back?"

"Yeah, sure. 'Scuse me, ladies. Duty calls." He winked at Patrice and lightly chucked Desiree under the chin. "See you in a bit."

Patrice watched him walk away. "Your brother sure is something. Long, lean and gorgeous."

"You say that every time you see him."

"Can't help it, it's true."

The waitress put their drinks on the bar.

"I have a table but we can sit here if you want," said Patrice.

"I'm staying long enough to hear Rafe and then I'm heading home."

"Are you going to tell him what happened?"

"I'm thinking about it. But you know Rafe. He'll find Max and want to pull him apart. I don't need that. And Rafe can't afford any more headlines. His motorcycle accident a few months back was sufficient, not to mention all the women he's always linked up with."

"Have it your way," Patrice conceded, taking a sip of her martini. "But you be careful."

The spotlight hit the stage and the band began to play.

Spence stood at the door of the kitchen, hoping to catch a glimpse of Desiree. At least she wasn't here with that Max guy. Thinking about that brought back the avalanche of events. His seeing Desiree with Max had sent him on a stupid drinking binge that had Michelle in his house in her underwear, that led to their falling-out and her not showing up for work for two days.

She'd finally returned his calls and told him that she needed to take some time off. A week, maybe longer. And since the staff was cross-trained, she was sure that Nichole could handle things in her absence. He'd tried to get her to talk but she'd refused. Told him there was nothing to talk about. It sounded very final in more ways than one and he wondered if Michelle would decide to come back at all.

He blew out a breath of resignation. What a mess. And he had no one to blame but himself. He caught sight of Desiree and watched the way she held her glass, the way her neck arched when she laughed, the look of pride on her face as she listened to her brother play.

Spence turned away and went back into the kitchen. He was going to get Desiree Lawson out of his system once and for all.

After the set, Rafe and Spence set an official date for him to perform at Bottoms Up. Rafe, Desiree and Patrice said their good-nights to Spence and stepped out into the late evening.

The moment Desiree stepped outside, that eerie sensation settled over her. She took her brother's arm.

"Where are you ladies parked?"

"I'm right across the street," Patrice said.

"Me, too."

They walked with Patrice to her car.

"Take my advice," Patrice said into Desiree's ear as they hugged. "Tell him."

"No," she whispered back and kissed her cheek. "Talk to you tomorrow."

Rafe and Desiree waited until Patrice pulled off, then walked to Desiree's car.

"You seem a little edgy," Rafe said as they walked to her car. "Everything okay?"

"Yes, everything is fine." She squeezed his arm.

He glanced at her. "You know you can tell me."

She looked up at him. "Everything is fine. Honest."

They stopped in front of her car. "When are you coming by the house?" She disengaged the alarm.

"Soon."

"Promise?"

"Promise." He kissed her cheek and she got in. "Drive safely."

"I will." She shut the door and started the car.

Rafe turned and walked around the corner to where he was parked. Desiree thought to stop him and tell him what had transpired but changed her mind, pulled off and headed home.

Chapter 12

The moment Desiree stepped in the house, she went in search of her sister. She didn't care what kind of agreement they'd made. The deal was off.

She knocked on Dominique's door.

"Come in."

Desiree opened the door. Dominique was propped up on her bed, chatting on the phone. When she saw the look on her sister's face, she cut her conversation short. "Let me call you back." She disconnected the call. "What's wrong?"

Desiree crossed the room and sat down in a club chair opposite Dominique's queen-size bed.

She told her what had transpired at her office, the chill she felt and how she was an inch away from reporting it to the police. The only thing stopping her was having the family name in the papers, which in all likelihood would happen.

For a long while Dominique, who had an answer for everything, was speechless. She scooted to the edge of the bed. "Desi, I am so sorry. I had no idea, I swear to you."

"I'm not saying it's your fault. But this is it, Dom. No more blind dates, hookups, whatever. I was perfectly happy and should have never agreed to this in the first place." She hugged herself, remembering the dark look in Max's eyes. "It was like he was a different person or something," she said, looking off into a space that only she could see. She shook her head, then focused on Dominique. "So this is it. Got it?"

Dominique nodded. "Sure. Okay. I was only trying to help."

Desiree stood. "See you in the morning. I'm going to bed."

As Desiree lay in bed, staring up at the ceiling, Patrice's comment echoed in her head. *If you'd just told Spence how you feel, none of this would have happened.*

Spence was settling down for the evening, listening to some music to unwind, when the phone rang.

"Hello."

"Spence, it's me, Dom."

"Dom, what is it? Are you crying?"

"Can I come over?"

"Sure, baby. What's wrong?"

"I really messed up this time. I'll tell you about it when I get there."

"All right. Listen, take it easy on the road. I'll leave the door open. Let yourself in."

"Okay," she sniffed.

Spence frowned as he slowly hung up the phone. What in the world could have happened? Little to nothing rocked Dominique. So whatever it was had to be serious.

He went into the kitchen and poured himself a glass of pomegranate juice, leaned against the sink and drank, his thoughts going in a million different directions at once.

He sighed heavily, put the glass in the sink and went into the living room to wait on Dominique. He pointed the remote at the television and turned it on. No use in speculating. He'd simply have to wait and see what she had to say.

Desiree heard the front door open, then close. She shifted in her bed. Then the sound of a car engine starting pulled her out of bed. She went to the window that faced the front of the house. Dominique was pulling out of the driveway. Desiree frowned. Where was she going this time of night? she wondered as she got back in bed. Probably some late-night date. She pulled the covers up to her chin and settled down again. Justin was on campus until the weekend. Dom had gone who knows where. She blinked against the night. She was alone and every sound that the generations-old mansion made seemed amplified.

* * *

Dominique let herself into Spence's house, as she'd done on many occasions. Spence had always been there for her. Their friendship was the one thing she could always depend on no matter what. It could have been more. They could have crossed the line, but they never had. Sometimes she'd wish that they did.

She shut the door behind her and locked it and came down the short hall that opened to his living room. The off-white walls showcased an array of framed photos, from the stars who had performed at Bottoms Up to pictures of him and his buddy Dexter to shots of Spence and Dominique at a party they'd attended years earlier.

Spence got up from the couch when he heard the front door and met her halfway. She walked into his arms and rested her head on his chest. He gathered her close, then put his arm around her waist and ushered her inside.

"Sit. Can I get you anything?"

She shook her head.

He lowered himself onto the space next to her on the couch. "Talk to me."

She laid her head on his shoulder and between stopping and starting she told him all about her brilliant plan to set her sister up with the perfect guy and the fiasco it turned out to be.

Spence's head was pounding. It was Dom who'd been setting Desiree up with dates? And that bastard Max... He couldn't get his thoughts straight.

"She's so pissed at me." She sniffed. "And I don't

know what to do about Max. He turned out to be a real creep. I have to find a way to make it up to her."

His body stiffened. "Make it up to her? How? By finding some other nut for her to go out with? Don't you think you've done enough?" He pulled away and stood, went to the bar and started to fix a drink, then changed his mind.

Dominique sat up on the couch. "What the hell is wrong with you?" She wiped her eyes. "I'm the one that's upset."

"Dom, this isn't about you. Everything can't be about you. Don't you get it?"

She jumped to her feet. "You're supposed to be my friend. I came here because I thought you would understand!"

"What is there to understand? You do what you always do, try to manipulate people, twist them around your pretty little finger, and this time it backfired big-time."

Her eyes widened with shock. "Manipulate people? That's what you think of me?" Her voice rose with every word. She swung toward the couch, snatched up her purse and went storming down the hall.

Spence stopped her at the door. "Relax." He gently put his hand on her shoulder. "You know good and well I'm not going to let you go flying out of here in the middle of the night with the mood you're in. Take yourself back inside and sit down."

"No," she said petulantly.

"Dom…"

She slowly turned around and looked up into his eyes. "Manipulative?" she said, sounding like a little girl.

He tried not to smile and nodded instead. "Very."

She blew out a breath and lowered her head.

"Come on, it's late. You can take my room. I'll crash on the couch."

"You sure?"

"Yeah, come on. You know where everything is." He walked with her up to his bedroom, grabbed a T-shirt from his dresser and a pair of pajama pants to sleep in.

"Night." He kissed the top of her head.

"Night," she whispered, almost sounding contrite, but Spence knew better. If anything could get Dominique's juices going, it was defeat. That only made her more determined.

That was what he thought about as he tried to get comfortable on the couch. Dominique didn't like to lose. She was focused and determined, and if she was determined to set her sister up with who she thought was the perfect guy, not much could stop her, short of Desiree actually finding someone.

He should have told Dom how he felt about Desiree a long time ago, but with him and Dom being so close, close enough that they'd almost gone from BFFs to lovers, it felt awkward and messy.

He pressed his head down into the pillow. It was New Year's Eve about three years earlier. Dominique had had a big fight with her then boyfriend, some guy he couldn't even remember now, and she'd called him, crying on the phone, and asked him to come and keep her company. Spence agreed to swing by on his way to his own date.

When he arrived at the Lawson mansion, he found Dominique out on the balcony.

"Hey, babe."

"You came." She hurried to him and wrapped her arms around him. "I knew you would come." She took his hand and they walked over to the balcony edge.

It was an exquisite night in Louisiana. The air was cool. The sky was brilliantly lit with hundreds of stars. The excitement of a new year had charged the atmosphere.

They sipped champagne as Dominique told him about the silly argument that had totally been blown out of proportion and had left her dateless on the biggest night of the year.

They laughed and talked and drank some more and then the sky lit up with an explosion of fireworks. Dominique leaped to her feet, her face was radiant under the lights, her eyes filled with joy and all he could see was Desiree. He wanted to take her in his arms right at that moment. An instant of indecision passed between both of them as they stared into each other's eyes. That would have been the biggest mistake of his life.

"Happy New Year's," he'd said and kissed her on her cheek.

He made up his mind that from that day on he and Dominique would always be friends and no more.

He'd tried everything to get Desiree out of his head, from a parade of women to even using Melanie Harte's Platinum Society's elite dating service. Nothing had worked. But now that Dominique was on a one-woman matchmaking campaign, he knew that his time of standing platonically on the sidelines would have to end.

Desiree was walking out of the door to leave for work and ran right into Dominique.

"Well, good morning. Where did you spend the night?"

"Spence's house."

Desiree's expression remained passive while her insides knotted. "Oh."

Dominique took her sister's hand. "I'm really sorry about what happened. I'll make it up to you, I swear. And if Max DeLaine ever comes near you again…"

Desiree squeezed her sister's hand. "All is forgiven. Forget it. Please. Look, I'm going to be late for a meeting. I'll see you later." She brushed by her and trotted down the steps that led to the path to the driveway and tried not to think about Spence and her sister spending the night together.

Dominique stood at the door for a moment, then closed it behind her. It wasn't all right and it wouldn't be until she fixed it. At least she had a plan B.

When Spence returned to work, he was surprised and relieved to find Michelle at her desk in the back office.

He stuck his head in the partially opened door. "Hey. Can I come in?"

Michelle tucked her hair behind her ears and put down her pen. "Hi. Sure. Come in."

He stepped in, feeling almost as if he was stepping into a lion's den. He kept the door open. "Good to see you back."

She linked her fingers together, glanced down, then directly at Spence. "What happened…it was silly and impulsive." She looked away. "You were right. Whatever there was between us was over a long time ago." She focused back on Spence. "I don't want what happened the other night to come between us." Her eyes filled and she quickly blinked away the impending tears.

"Neither do I, Chell. You're important to me. I think you know that."

She nodded.

Spence drew in a breath of relief. "So we're cool?"

A tight smile tugged at her mouth. "Yes, we're cool."

"Good to have you back," he said and slipped out.

For the first time in days he felt like a weight was off of his chest, he thought as he prepared his seasonings for crawfish stew. One thing had been settled. Now his next hurdle was what he was going to do about Desiree. One thing he was certain of was that he couldn't give Dominique another chance at her crazy plan. He needed to be in the running. He needed to make sure that Desiree knew how he felt and then hope for the best.

"Why do you need Melanie Harte's number?" Rafe asked while he popped a bagel in the toaster. He turned to his sister, who'd shown up at his door unannounced—as usual. Fortunately, he was alone.

Dominique gave him her best little sister smile.

"Her grandmother fixed up Daddy and Mama. And if I remember right, Daddy got you set up, too."

"Yeah, the old man's idea, not mine. Remember?" A shadow of a smile lifted his mouth. "Although I must admit that meeting Melanie Harte was a bonus." He focused on his sister. "And…you still haven't answered my question. What are you up to now?"

She spun slowly from side to side in the swivel bar stool at the island counter.

Rafe opened the fridge and took out a carton of orange juice. "I'm listening, Dom, and it better be good."

"Okay…you beat it out of me. I promised Desi that I would find the perfect guy for her. I'm tired of seeing her work, work and never have any fun. She hasn't had a serious relationship with anyone since what's-his-name. And that was ages ago. And then the whole Max fiasco…" She caught herself but it was too late.

Rafe swung toward her. "What Max fiasco?"

"It's really no big deal. Honest."

"What happened, Dominique? And you better tell me the truth."

She exhaled. "All right, all right." With great reluctance she confessed to her brother what she'd been up to and what had transpired between Max and Desiree.

Rafe's jaw was clenched so tight that Dominique was sure he was going to crack his teeth.

His expression was like stone. "Did he touch her?"

"No. She swore to me that he didn't."

He took a step toward her. "Are you lying to me, Dom?"

"No. Honest." Her heart pounded.

He stormed past her.

"Where are you going?"

"You can let yourself out." He grabbed his keys from the small table in the hall and the next sound she heard was the roar of his Harley as he tore out of his driveway.

"Damn. That didn't go well." She hopped down from the stool and had every intention of leaving and praying for the best when Rafe's open door to his office seemed to beckon her.

She went inside and looked around. Maybe he had a card lying around somewhere. She peeked in his desk drawer and flipped through an old appointment book, and lo and behold, there was Melanie's number penned in for a time when he'd apparently gone up to visit her a year earlier. She jotted down the number and slid the book back in the desk just the way she'd found it. She grinned, utterly pleased with herself and thankful that her brother still believed in having a backup plan after having lost his cell phone at one time and all the information in it.

Dominique stepped outside and locked the front door behind her. Maybe her day wouldn't be so bad, after all, and hopefully her hotheaded brother wouldn't do anything stupid. She hurried to her office. She had some quick work to do.

Desiree was gathering up her notes for a meeting, knowing that the long debate ahead would keep her mind off of Dominique and Spence, when her office door opened and Rafe took up all the space.

"Rafe. This is a surprise. What are you doing here?" Her smile of greeting slowly faded when she saw the storm brewing behind his dark eyes.

He closed the door.

"What's wrong?"

"That's what I want you to tell me."

"I don't know what you mean."

"No use in hiding it from me. Dom already told me."

She sank back into her seat, pushed out a breath and squeezed her eyes shut for a moment. She was eventually going to have to kill her sister. "What did she say?"

"I want to hear your side first and then I want you to tell me why you didn't say a word to me."

"I didn't tell you, because you would act like this."

"Like what? Like a man looking out for his family like a man is supposed to do, not like some creep who follows women around and threatens them."

She held up her hand. "Wait. He didn't threaten me."

"His presence did. Now, tell me what happened."

She lowered her head into her hands, then looked across at her scowling brother and told him everything.

When she finished he stopped pacing.

"You said he works at Southern University," he said, a little too calm for Desiree's taste. "I may have to pay him a visit during his office hours."

"Raford James Lawson. You are not going to that man's job." She pushed back from her desk and stood.

"Just a little friendly visit. Man-to-man. Straighten a few things out."

"Rafe." She came from behind her desk and clasped his hard upper arm. "Please. Don't do anything stupid. Let it go. Please. For my sake. Do it for me."

He bent down and kissed her cheek. He couldn't stand it when his sisters would put that pained look in their eyes. They knew it could bend him to their will. "I'll talk to you later." He turned and walked out.

She slowly shook her head in frustration. Yes, she was definitely going to have to kill her sister. She returned to her desk, gathered her belongings and notes. She was heading for the door just as her phone started to ring. If she stopped now, she would be late for her meeting. Someone up front would get it or it would go to voice mail. She shut her office door and breezed out.

Lizzie waved goodbye and picked up the phone. "City council's office. How may I help you?"

"I was trying to reach Ms. Lawson."

"I'm sorry. She's out of the office for the rest of the day. Can someone else help you? Or can I take a message?"

"No. Thanks." Spence hung up the phone.

Chapter 13

"I totally understand," Dominique was saying into the phone. "I want it to be a surprise for my sister. A birthday present." She scrunched her face up against the lie.

"Send all the info over, along with a recent picture, and we'll do a preliminary workup. Come up with some possibilities."

"Thank you so much, Melanie. You're a doll."

"The only reason I'm doing this is because of my grandmother and your parents…and that handsome brother of yours. Has he settled down any?"

Dominique laughed. "Rafe, not likely. I'll get everything over to you this afternoon."

"Fine."

Dominique hung up, totally satisfied with herself.

She'd make it up to her sister by finding her the perfect guy and then all would really be forgiven.

Desiree was exhausted by the time she finished up with her round of meetings. By the time she arrived home, all she could think about was a hot bath and a good night's sleep. She pulled her car into her spot in the driveway and went inside. The last person she wanted to deal with was her sister. She wasn't in the frame of mind to hear any of her excuses or listen to any of her sweet talk. She'd really crossed the line this time by telling Rafe. All day she'd been expecting to hear a news blast that her brother had done something crazy and it would be all Dominique's fault.

She put her key in the door and sighed in relief at the silence. Maybe Dominique had gone to spend the night with Spence again. She didn't care anymore. It didn't matter. Whatever silly idea she had about her and Spence was a waste of good energy. Tomorrow she'd take her frustration out on the track.

She climbed the stairs and went down the long hallway to her bedroom. Passing her sister's door, she saw a light from underneath. For a moment she stopped, thought about giving her a piece of her mind, but decided against it and kept walking to her room. She'd had enough aggravation for one day.

Once inside the sanctuary of her bedroom she peeled off her clothes and went straight for the bathroom. She turned on the tub and added her favorite scent. Soon the room was filled with the soothing aroma of jasmine. Just as she was about to get in, the house phone rang. Dom would get it, she thought. But it kept ringing.

She pulled her robe around her and went out in the hallway and picked up the phone on the table by the stairs. The only person who ever called on the house line was her father. It was late, especially for her father. She hoped nothing was wrong.

"Hello, Daddy?"

"No. Actually it's not."

Desiree frowned. "Spence?"

"Yes, hi."

Her heart pounded. "Um, hi. Hang on. I'll get Dom."

"No. Wait. I actually called to speak with you."

"Me?"

"Yes." He hesitated. "I…I called your office today but I'd just missed you."

He wasn't making sense. "I don't understand…."

"I know and I'm not making this any clearer. I'm calling because…I should have called ages ago. I should have told you how I felt long before now."

Her body began to tremble. She gripped the phone. "Felt…about what?"

"About you."

She leaned against the wall. Her heart was racing so fast she could barely breathe. This had to be one of her sister's crazy stunts.

"Look, I know this is out of the blue." He took a deep breath. "I was hoping that you'd have dinner with me."

"What?"

"Would you have dinner with me, or lunch or brunch or whatever?"

"I…"

"Just say yes. We can go wherever you want."

"I don't understand….You and Dom…"

"What about me and Dom?"

"You two…"

"Oh." He blew out a breath. "There's nothing going on with me and Dom, never has been. Is that what you… Look, we can talk about all of that. We can talk about whatever you want." He waited.

Desiree gripped the phone even tighter. This was some kind of dream. It didn't make sense. A million questions were running around in her head at once. Her stomach swirled.

"I have plans for tomorrow."

"Oh…"

"But if you want, you can come along," she said, the words flowing from her and taking on a life of their own. "I'm going into N'Awlins around ten."

"How about if I drive you?"

"Okay."

"I'll be by to pick you up at eight."

"I'll be out front."

"See you then. Good night, Desi."

"Good night." She hung up the phone and in a daze she returned to her room; her bath forgotten. Once she shut the door behind her, she had to cover her mouth to muffle her screams of joy. She danced in circles of disbelief. Had he really called and said he wanted to see her? *Her?* That there was nothing going on between him and her sister—ever? Could she believe that? She wanted to, needed to. This was the moment she'd dreamed of, that one day, Spence Hampton would see her and not her sister.

She pressed her hands to her chest and closed her eyes, then darted across the room and snatched up her cell phone. She punched in Patrice's number and hoped that she was still up and free to talk.

"Trice…you'll never guess who called me!"

They talked for over an hour, with Patrice grilling her for every single detail. Then she made her tell it all again.

"Well, it's about damned time is all I have to say. I told you he had a thing for you."

"No, you didn't."

"I should have. Anyway, I guess I can sleep late tomorrow since Mr. Hampton will be accompanying you to the track. Did you tell him where you were going?"

"No."

"Ha, that's gonna be a surprise."

"He likes cars. He rebuilds them."

"Liking cars, rebuilding them and then seeing the woman you're taking out for the first time behind the wheel, going one hundred seventy-five miles an hour, is a whole different thing."

"Maybe you're right."

"Look, I haven't been right about much of anything lately. So don't go by me. Besides, this will definitely be a test. If he can handle it, then the rest is gravy."

Desiree grinned. "Yeah. It will be."

"Get some rest. I have a feeling you're going to need it."

* * *

Desiree was up with the sun. She'd barely slept, and when she did, her dreams were filled with images, sounds and scents of Spence. When she opened her eyes for a moment, she thought that maybe it was all a dream, that the phone call had never happened. She jumped out of bed and went to the phone in the hall. She pressed caller ID and the number for Bottoms Up appeared in the illuminated dial. The funny flutter in the center of her stomach went crazy. She darted back to her room just as Dominique came out of hers.

They faced each other.

Dominique had an overnight bag on her shoulder and a carry-on at her feet. "Hope I didn't wake you."

"No. I was up. Coming or going?"

"Going actually. To Acapulco for a long weekend with some friends. I'll be back on Monday morning. I should have told you."

"You're a big girl. You don't have to tell me everything. Have a nice time. Safe travels and try to behave yourself."

"That takes all the fun out of a mini vacation." She crossed the short space and stood in front of her mirror image. "I know you're still upset. And Rafe told me that he came to your office, and I know this whole mess is my fault. But I swear to you, I will make it up to you."

"Dom, forget it. It's over. Okay. Go have a good time."

"Will you be okay here all alone? Call Trice and tell her to come over for the weekend."

"Um, I'll be fine. Really."

"Sure?"

"Positive."

A car horn blew.

"That's Zoie. We have a 9:00 a.m. flight. Gotta run." She kissed Desiree's cheek. "Love you."

"You, too."

She watched Dominique trot down the stairs and out of the house, listened for the car to pull off before she breathed a sigh of relief. She was hoping to be able to ease by without Dom seeing her get into Spence's car. That was one less thing to worry about. If this was any indication of the rest of her day, then it was going to be pretty good.

Desiree darted back to her room. It was already seven. Spence would be here in an hour. "Spence will be here in an hour," she said out loud and then pinched herself. She shook her head, looked around the room and suddenly the always organized, clearheaded Desiree Janel Lawson was all aflutter, a complete basket case. What should she wear? Should she dress up, dress down? What scent should she put on? She should have had her nails done. But she didn't have time. He called only last night. Last night Spence Hampton called her! She looked around her room, turned in a circle and finally focused on finding something to wear.

She decided on a pair of steel-gray linen pants, nicely lined to keep them from wrinkling, a soft dove-gray silk blouse with a two-foot-long silver chain that she draped in several rows around her neck. Although she was only five-five and generally opted for heels, today she wore her favorite pair of black flats with an innersole that felt like heaven. She could walk for days in those shoes. She applied lip gloss with a hint of color and some mascara to emphasize her eyes. She ran her fingers through her wild curls so that her hair was a halo around her face.

With only ten minutes to spare, Desiree declared herself ready, at least, that is, until she heard a car pull into the driveway, the engine shut off and the front doorbell ring. Heat rushed through her and her stomach did a complete three-sixty. Her hands shook as she grabbed the banister and went downstairs.

She stood in front of the door, tugged in a long breath, willed herself to be calm and opened the door.

She froze. "What are you doing here?"

"I just wanted to talk," Max said.

"Please leave. Now."

"Come on, Desiree, hear me out. Please."

"Goodbye, Max." She tried to push the door and he pushed back. She stumbled, holding on to the knob for support.

"Get out!" She shoved the door again. Real fear and fury filled her veins.

"Hey!"

They both turned at the sound of the heavy baritone.

"You heard the lady." Spence took the last of the steps and stood between Desiree and Max. He threw her a quick look. "You all right?"

She nodded numbly, not even realizing when Spence had arrived.

"Do like the lady said and leave. Now."

"I just wanted to talk to her."

"She's not talking today. How's that? So we can do this the easy way, and you can walk away on your own, or we can do it the hard way and *I* can make you leave, or we can do it the legal way and have the police come and get you." He took a step closer to Max. "Your choice."

Max tried to catch a glimpse of Desiree, who was blocked from head to toe by Spence's body. "I don't want any trouble. I only wanted to talk to her. That's all."

"Like I said, not today. And not any other day unless she says so. Got it?"

Max tugged on his sports jacket and straightened himself up. "Fine." He turned and walked down the steps and to his car.

Spence didn't budge until he was sure that Max DeLaine was long gone. He turned to Desiree. His brows were knitted tightly together as his gaze ran across her face and up and down her body. He clasped her forearms, looked down into her eyes. "Are you sure you're okay? Did he touch you?"

"I'm fine. Really." This was the second time in days that a man had come to her rescue about Max DeLaine.

"Are you sure?"

"Yes. I'm sure," she snapped, the appearance of Max had set her nerves on edge. "I appreciate the chivalry but I'm not some damsel in distress. I can take care of myself."

Spence held up his hands, palms open. A soft smile of acquiescence moved across his mouth. "I believe you."

Desiree lowered her head for a moment and briefly shut her eyes before looking at him. "Please…come in."

She stepped aside and Spence stepped into the house he'd visited a million times, but never to see Desiree. She shut the door and locked it.

He turned, shoved his hands in the pockets of his khaki slacks and faced her.

"You make a great entrance," she said, the light of merriment dancing in her eyes.

Spence laughed, the moment of tension between them bursting like a pricked balloon. "We all have our charms."

"I didn't mean to snap at you."

"It's cool. Heat of the moment." He waited. "You want to tell me what that was all about?"

Desiree pushed out a breath. "On the ride over to N'Awlins."

"Fair enough. Seems like we have a lot to talk about."

Her gaze jumped to his. The reality of what had transpired only last night and the reason for him being there were things she was still trying to process.

"Ready?"

"My bag is upstairs. I'll be right back." She headed toward the stairs.

"The forecast is for late showers, maybe a thunderstorm," he called out after her.

"Okaaaay."

Moments later Desiree was back with a leather carry-all that contained her racing clothes, shoes, her helmet, a towel and toiletries.

Spence glanced curiously at the bag. "Big bag. I can take it for you." He reached for it and his hand brushed hers. Electric heat scurried up her arm. Her heart thumped.

"I got it," she said, hoping she didn't sound as breathless as she suddenly felt. She hefted the bag onto her shoulder.

"Looks heavy. What are you planning on doing in the Big Easy, anyway?" He unlocked the front door and pulled it open.

She tucked in her smile and set the alarm. "You'll see." She brushed by him, caught a hint of his cologne, which made her want to bury her face in his neck and snuggle there.

"Can't wait." He shut the door behind them and watched her move sensuously and as undulating as the Mississippi and he wondered how long he would be able to keep from doing to her all the things he'd been fantasizing about. When he said "Can't wait," he meant it in more ways than one.

Chapter 14

"This is a beauty," Desiree said with awe as she ran her hand across the hood of the Mustang. "Nineteen seventy-eight, right?"

His brow rose in surprise. "On the button." He opened the passenger door for her.

"What can she do fully opened? One-ten, one-fifteen?"

"One-twenty."

She nodded in admiration and slid onto the cool white leather seat and fastened her belt.

Spence settled in and turned the key in the ignition. The engine hummed to life, bringing a smile to Desiree's lips.

"V-eight engine. Four cylinders."

"If you wanted to impress me, you have." He drove the car out of the driveway and onto the road and headed toward New Orleans. For a while they drove in a comfortable silence. The sounds of businesses opening, joggers and dog walkers, and the music of the early morning birds filled the space between them.

Spence forced himself to concentrate on the road and not steal glances at the rise and fall of Desiree's breasts with every breath she took, or fixate on the way her scent had invaded his senses and was making him crazy. He gripped the steering wheel. They came to a red light.

"What made you say yes?" he asked.

The unexpected resonance of his voice tingled, then penetrated deep down to her center, spread and warmed her to the tips of her fingers.

He watched the tiny pulse beat in her throat and longed to put his lips there.

Her eyes played with his, then danced away. She had a million answers and none at all. Could she tell him that she'd dreamed of this day, that he'd been a part of her thoughts and fantasies for as long as she cared to remember?

"I'm not sure, really." She thought about the words, which sat so heavy on her tongue, the tiny lie she'd just told. She glanced down at her hands, which were folded on her lap. "I…wanted to see you, too."

A smile moved up from the center of his chest and eased across his mouth like daybreak, slow and bright. "You don't know how bad I needed to hear you say that."

They jumped at the blare of a car horn that sounded off behind them.

Spence reached across the gearshift and squeezed her hand.

Desiree held his gaze for a moment and her heart felt as if it would leap out of her chest. Was she grinning as hard as she thought she was?

The horn sounded again. Spence put the car in gear and took off across the intersection, took the next exit and headed for the highway.

"So you think I had a thing with your sister, huh?" He kept his eyes on the road.

"Who wouldn't? The two of you were always…so close."

He stole a quick glance at Desiree. "I'm crazy for your sister. But not like that. To be honest, part of the reason I hung around was because I'd hope to see you. But you never gave me the time of day."

"What!" she said in disbelief.

He bobbed his head. "Yep. Totally ignored me."

She angled her body to face him and studied his rugged profile, the strong jaw, the slight shadow of a beard, the outline of his full bottom lip, the angle of his nose, the curve of his brow, the coffee bean brown of his skin. She thought she'd memorized him from every angle, but today, without the inhibition of having to pretend that she didn't care, she was seeing him in a new way. She was seeing him with promise in her eyes, not with the futility that had clouded her vision before.

"What took you so long to say something?" she asked, feeling bold.

"Let's say I didn't want my ego crushed."

She waved a hand in dismissal. "I don't believe that."

"It's true." He turned to her and winked.

"Hmm, just like I thought," she teased, getting more comfortable with Spence by the minute. "You wanted to know why I said yes, but why did you finally decide to chance getting your ego hurt?"

He pulled up behind a line of cars merging onto the exit ramp. "When Dominique told me that she'd been trying to hook you up with the perfect guy...I knew that if I didn't make a move...I couldn't let you get away." He took a quick look at her and sank into the depths of her eyes.

"Maybe Dom got her wish, anyway," she said softly.

The corners of his eyes crinkled when he smiled. "I'll have to personally thank her."

He headed onto the ramp leading into New Orleans. "You want to tell me what the deal is with that Max creep?" He jaw tightened just thinking about him. He stared straight ahead, then took a quick look at Desiree when she didn't respond.

"Dom introduced us...at the get-together at the house."

He nodded.

"He seemed nice enough, even though I had my reservations. We went to dinner at Mansur...."

He remembered all too well but held his tongue.

She folded and unfolded her hands. "He showed up at my office."

"He did what?"

Desiree held her breath a moment, then nodded yes. "We talked briefly. He left, at least I thought he did." She ran her hands up and down her arms. "When I came out, he…he was there, right in front of me. He started saying he just wanted to talk to me." She remembered how frightened she'd been and now reliving it only made the chill return…and then today. She gave a little shiver.

He slammed his palm against the steering wheel. "You should have reported him."

"It's complicated."

"It needs to get uncomplicated, Desi. This is not something to be taken lightly."

She sighed. "I know," she said, her voice a whisper as the reality of the latest run-in resurfaced. "I know."

They drove in silence for a while; the music of Kem played seductively through the car stereo speakers. His soothing melodies seemed to unfurl the tension that had sprung up between them. Spence hummed along and Desiree bobbed her head. Spence hit the last note in a perfect off-key fashion and they both cracked up laughing.

Desiree's eyes sparkled. "Guess we won't be taking that show on the road."

Spence chuckled. "I don't think so." He paused a moment. "Can I have a hint as to where we're going?"

"I'm, um, going to the racetrack."

"The racetrack? Really?" His brows rose and fell. "I didn't take you for a betting kinda girl."

She tucked in her smile. "Hmm, there's a lot you don't know about me, Mr. Hampton."

"That's what I'm here to find out."

They slipped back into an easy comfort, talking about the upcoming elections, the restaurant, her days at the city council office, her older sister's marriage, Spence's love for restoring cars.

"You could really go into business for yourself."

"I like it as a hobby. I really don't want the pressure and demands of clients. This way I work within my own time frame and do things how I want."

Desiree nodded in understanding. "That makes sense. There's nothing like doing what you love."

"Do you love working at the city council?"

She smiled and turned halfway toward him. "Actually I do. Some days it's overwhelming and exhausting and you feel as though you will never be able to move the mountain. But then you start taking away the dirt and the rocks a little bit at a time. The way government works or doesn't," she said, tongue in cheek, "has always intrigued me. My father still has it in his head that Rafe will one day shake off his wanderlust and take up the mantle."

In unison they said, "Not gonna happen," then cracked up laughing.

"You think you'd ever get more involved in politics… run for office?" he asked.

"I don't know. The opportunity hasn't presented itself."

"What if it did?"

"That's something that I would consider." She adjusted herself in her seat. "Unlike my brother or Dom, politics are in my blood and Lee Ann's as well. Had Lee Ann not taken over our mother's role when she passed, and then become my father's assistant, I'm pretty sure she would have run for office, at least on the local level."

"What about Justin?"

"I could very well see him throwing his hat in the ring in a few years. He wants to get his law degree and after that I think he will be ready to make some decisions about career choices."

"Well, since Justin's name is on the table…is he seeing anyone?"

Her brows drew together. "Why?"

"Have you ever met Nichole? She's one of the assistants at the restaurant."

Desiree was thoughtful for a moment. "Hmm, not sure. What does she look like?"

"Petite, but a pretty close ringer for that model… what's-her-name."

Desiree's expression brightened with recognition. "Yes, yes, I know exactly who you're talking about."

"Naomi Campbell," they chorused in harmony and chuckled at having once again read each other's thoughts.

"Okay. What about her?"

"Well…" He took the exit ramp toward the track. They were about five minutes away. "She wanted me to introduce her to Justin."

"Really." She was quiet for a minute.

"Bad idea?"

"At the moment I have a bad taste in my mouth about setups. I'm probably not the best person to ask."

"Hmm," he murmured, conceding his blunder.

"If it helps any, he's not seeing anyone at the moment.

Maybe the next time we have something happening at the house, you can invite her."

"I'll keep that in mind."

The entrance to the track loomed ahead.

"The parking lot is to your left," she said.

Spence turned the car in the direction of the lot and found a space among the hundred or so cars that were already there.

"Looks like it's filling up pretty early," he said, locking up the Mustang.

Desiree tugged her bag onto her shoulder and began walking toward the entrance. "This way."

Spence caught up and walked alongside her. "What's in that bag, anyway?"

"Stuff."

He glanced at her and grinned. "Stuff…"

Desiree walked toward the seating area and climbed up the steps to the center rows.

"Is this where you usually sit?" He shrugged out of his jacket and tossed it across the back of the seat.

Desiree's breath caught when she glimpsed the expanse of his chest beneath the fitted T-shirt. "Um, sort of."

"Are you being intentionally mysterious?" He pulled his sunglasses from his jacket pocket and put them on.

"Make yourself comfortable. I'll be back."

"But…"

Desiree hurried away. If she wanted to get in on the first round, she had about ten minutes to sign in and change. She darted beneath the track seating and down the long tunnel to the dressing and preparation room. She pushed open the heavy door and was immediately filled with a rush of adrenaline. Drivers were in their gear. She could hear the roar of engines and the cacophony of voices from the pit shouting out orders. The smell of gasoline filled her nostrils.

"Hey, D.J.," Vinny, one of the drivers, called out. "Driving today?"

"You know I am." She waved to a few other familiar faces and hurried toward the check-in desk.

"Hey, D.J."

"Hey, Martha." She flipped through the log and signed her name. "Is my team ready?"

"Down in the pit, fueling the Ferrari. Slotted you in for second today," she said in her raspy voice, which sounded like something from a bad B movie. "You won't have to wait long, so you better get ready." She blew a puff of smoke in the air and stubbed out her cigarette in the overflowing ashtray.

"Thanks, Martha. You're the best."

Martha Wisdom was as much a fixture of the track and racing life as the warning flags and the finish line. Rumor had it that the track and the entire enterprise were actually hers, but she was so eccentric that she pretended to be this poor middle-aged woman who needed a job and loved cars. Desiree had seen her down in the pit, under the hoods of more cars than she could remember. Martha definitely knew her stuff. And if the rumor was true…well, then, more power to her!

Desiree wove her way in and out of the drivers and mechanics until she reached the end of the hallway. She greeted a few of the guys, found her locker and did a quick change. Moments later she emerged from the tunnel and headed to the pit where her precious Ferrari awaited.

"Hey, guys."

"Got her all ready for you," Al said, wiping the grease from his hands with an old rag, which he then stuffed into the pocket of his overalls.

The rest of the pit team finished tightening the lugs on the wheels and Al shut the hood.

Desiree secured the chin strap from her helmet and got in behind the wheel.

Spence couldn't imagine what was taking Desiree so long and why she was being so mysterious. He surveyed the wide track in front of him, the concession stand, tried to spot her among the growing number of people who were seated in the stands but saw no signs of her. Not to mention that he was getting the impression that this wasn't actual racing at all. He didn't see any cars lining up on the track. In all the time he'd been sitting there, the announcer had called out one name and given a blow-by-blow of the escalating speeds of the one driver as he sped around the track.

What was going on? He settled back down in his seat. Maybe this was all the warm-up and the real racing would be starting soon.

And then he went completely still when he heard the name D. J. Lawson blared over the loudspeaker. Coincidence that Desiree and the driver would have the same last name, he told himself. But where the hell was Desiree?

The Ferrari was pushed by the crew to the starting line. Desiree strapped herself in and turned on the engine. Her pulse escalated with the rumble of the engine when it kicked on and then the comforting purr that followed. She checked all her indicator lights, revved the engine and waited for the flag. The trip around the track was only ten minutes, but it was the most exhilarating, most liberating ten minutes of her life.

The flag dropped and she was off.

That Ferrari was a real beauty, Spence thought as he watched its sleek body practically blur as the driver accelerated the speed. He watched in awe and admiration as the driver handled the curves with ease, even as the announcer said the car was approaching 110 miles per hour, 115, 120, 130.

Man, what he wouldn't give for a chance to really open up and fly like that. He stood with all the other spectators as they cheered the driver across the finish line. His heart was pumping, as if he'd been totally invested in the driver. He blew out a breath. Now he was getting worried. Where was Desiree? No way he could sit there any longer. He got up, took his jacket and followed the path that he'd seen Desiree take. With the incident at her house with that Max character in the back of his mind, his mild curiosity as to her whereabouts was turning into agitation.

He trotted down the stairs and followed a walkway that a bunch of other spectators were taking and somehow found himself in an overflowing lounge filled with drivers, mechanics, race car enthusiasts and the scent of gasoline and motor oil. The whole atmosphere gave him a rush of familiarity, as if this was a place that he had been looking for and had finally found. It was so odd. He couldn't shake the sensation and then there she was, coming toward him, chatting with another driver.

"Good luck," she said and gave him a thumbs-up.

"Great race today, D.J.," one of the drivers seated on a hard plastic chair called out as she passed.

D.J....what...?

She smiled her thanks and waved and then she spotted Spence staring at her in wide-eyed disbelief.

Her dimples flashed for a moment as she offered a sheepish grin. She walked up to him.

"Um, sorry I took so long."

He blinked several times, trying to merge what he thought he knew with what was actually going on in front of him. "You're D.J.? The driver that was behind the wheel of that magnificent Ferrari flying at one hundred thirty miles an hour?"

"Hey, D.J., great race," a passerby interrupted, clapping her on the shoulder before he sauntered off.

"Thanks, Paulie," she murmured. She turned her wide eyes of innocence on Spence. "That's me. D.J.," she said quietly. She took his arm. "Come on, let's go and I promise I will explain everything."

"Should I put you down for your usual time?" Martha asked as Desiree approached the desk.

"Yep, same time." She signed out. "Thanks, Martha. You take care of yourself."

"I will. Who's the handsome fella?" she asked, lifting her square chin in Spence's direction. "Ain't seen him around here before."

"Martha, this is Spence. Spence Hampton, Martha Wisdom."

Martha stuck out her thick hand. "So what do you think about your lady friend being one of the best drivers we got? She can beat some of these men around here with her eyes closed." She laughed a wet, raspy laugh. Her blue eyes crinkled at the corners.

Spence used the opportunity to put his arm possessively around Desiree's waist. "I tell you, D.J. is just full of surprises."

Once they were back out in the parking lot, Desiree tried to explain. "I should have told you," she began.

"Probably," he said with humor, opening the passenger side door. He came around to the other side and got in behind the wheel. He turned to her. "You wanna drive?" He held up the keys.

Desiree laughed. "I think I've filled my quota for today, but I would love to drive this baby at some point."

He stuck the key in the ignition. "Deal," he said as the engine came to life. He eased out of the parking lot and onto the road that led to the highway. "So tell me… how? and why? I would have never imagined this in a million years."

Desiree drew in a deep breath and slowly let it out. "I've had an interest in cars since I was a little girl," she began and went on to tell him about her secret passion and how her sister had dismissed it, telling her she'd never get a man with grease under her nails. They both laughed.

"So it became my secret. The only person who knows that I come down here is Patrice." She sighed, holding on to the last kernel of truth. "Driving, having something that's only for me, it gives me a sense of identity. It makes me separate from Dominique. Gives me a sense of control." She lowered her head for a moment. "I don't think anyone can truly understand what it's like to go through your entire life being compared to someone else."

She angled her body toward Spence. "Especially someone who looks exactly like you. They expect you to think the same and act the same and be the same. You have no identity. Who you are is tied to someone else." Her voice cracked in frustration. "I always felt that I was in Dom's large, all-encompassing shadow and that I would be there forever, that no one would ever really see me. Desiree Janel Lawson."

Spence reached over and covered her clasped hands with his. "I see you, Desi. I've always seen you. Now that I have the chance, I'm going to make sure that you know it. That's a promise."

Chapter 15

Desiree and Spence spent the drive back to Baton Rouge talking and laughing and filling in all the gaps. They realized that they knew so much about each other and then nothing at all. She loved art and he couldn't understand it. He loved to fish and she couldn't see herself hooking bait. They both enjoyed dancing and cooking and cars and traveling, and jazz and blues. She didn't realize that he was not a native of Louisiana but was born in Memphis and that was where his love of the blues came from. And it took him by surprise to discover that she had a storage room in the basement of the house that was filled with books—her other passion. She loved animals but everyone in the house was allergic except for her. Next to Dexter Beaumount, his best buddy was his dog, Howard.

"Your dog's name is Howard?" She couldn't stop laughing.

"Yep." He chuckled. "I wanted him to feel important," he said with a flourish. "No ordinary dog name for him."

"I've got to meet him. With a name like Howard I'm sure he has a great personality."

"That he does. Listen, I need to stop by the restaurant and check on a few things. Do you mind?"

"No. Not at all. I mean, if you want, you can drop me off at home."

They pulled up to a light. He turned to her. "Now that I finally have you with me, I don't intend to waste one minute apart."

The heat of his eyes played over her face. Her entire body tingled.

"That cool with you?"

All she could do was nod her head to make sure she didn't stir herself from this incredible dream she was having.

Spence parked in the space reserved for him behind Bottoms Up. The Saturday lunch crowd was in full swing when they walked in. Many of the tables were filled and the waitresses were busy completing orders.

"You have to be hungry," he said, with his hand at the small of her back.

His fingers seemed to sear through her clothes and spread to her limbs.

"I am, actually."

"Let me get you a table and you order what you want."

"Will you be able to join me?"

They'd stopped walking. Spence turned to face her. He looked down into her eyes. "I'll make that happen."

To Desiree, standing there looking at him, surrounded by him, everything else seemed to have vanished around her. She could feel his heartbeat and the electric energy that bounced off of him. She could see the light in his eyes and the way his mouth curved ever so slightly at the corners and she wanted to press her lips to his to see if they were as pillow soft as they looked.

Spence ran the pad of his thumb under her chin and swore he saw the tremor that he felt ripple through her. His insides strummed, as if his veins had turned into guitar strings and someone was playing an unfamiliar tune.

"Hey, Spence," Nichole greeted, breaking the spell. She turned her smile on Desiree. "Desiree, right?" she said with a bit of uncertainty.

Desiree smiled. "Yes. How are you?"

"Busy. But busy is good." She focused on Spence. "We weren't expecting you today."

"I thought I'd stop in and see how things were going."

Nichole put her hand on his arm. "You can take a day off, you know."

"So I've heard," he joked. "We're going to stay for

lunch. But I'm going to run in the kitchen for a minute. Could you get Desiree a table?"

"Sure. Follow me."

"I'll be right back," he said to Desiree and lightly kissed her cheek.

"Take your time. I'll be fine." She followed Nichole to a window table.

"How's this?"

"Perfect." She sat down.

"Do you want to order now or wait on Spence?"

"I'll wait."

"No problem. I'll send a server over shortly. Enjoy your meal." She hesitated a moment, then took the plunge. "Spence is really a great guy and it's good to see him with someone. I mean…he has this reputation of being a ladies' man, but he's not like that at all." She suddenly looked flustered. "I'm sorry. It's really none of my business. I better go before I really say something crazy."

"Um, Nichole…"

She stopped. "Yes?"

"The next time we have one of our parties at the house, I'd like you to come."

"Really?" Her whole face lit up as if someone had shone a light beneath her copper-colored complexion. "I'd love to."

Desiree grinned. "I'll be sure to let Spence know."

"Thank you, I'd like that." Nichole pressed her clipboard to her chest.

Desiree nodded.

"Well, I'd better get back to work." She practically skipped away.

Desiree got a good vibe from Nichole and maybe she would be someone that her brother Justin would be interested in. She picked up the menu and scanned the choices in the hopes of keeping her jangling stomach under control. She still felt as if she was living a dream. Being with Spence was what she'd imagined for years and now here she was and he was as wonderful as she'd always thought, and the day was still young.

After a leisurely lunch of stuffed crab and a house salad, Spence drove Desiree home. They sat parked on the driveway.

"Thank you for a wonderful day," Desiree said.

"I should be thanking you for saying yes." He looked into her expectant expression and the words tumbled out. "I don't want it to end. Not yet."

She was barely able to breathe over the pounding of her heart. "Dom is gone for the weekend. Justin is on campus. There's no chance that Rafe will drop by since he's so busy…." She let the invitation hang in the air.

"I was thinking the same thing."

The moment that was on the brink of taking them to the next step held them in its embrace.

"Why don't you come in?" she whispered. She opened her door and got out.

Spence took the keys from the ignition, grabbed her bag from the backseat and walked with her inside.

This time she let him carry her bag.

* * *

John Coltrane's "A Love Supreme" played in the background as they hummed and tapped their feet to the music, stretched out on deck chairs by the pool. It was nearly six and the temperature was still in the high eighties.

Desiree tried to keep her eyes on the calming waters and not on the ripples of Spence's chest or the way his swim trunks hung low on his pelvis.

The aroma of sizzling steak filled the air.

"I'm going to check on the steaks and take one more lap around the pool," Spence said, pushing up from his seat.

Desiree's eyes trailed him as he walked away and she did all she could not to lick her lips. She'd never been so nervous around a man before in her life, which was caused by long overdue desire that she had for him. What she wanted to do the moment they stepped across the threshold was take him straight to her bedroom and live out her fantasy. But Spence was being the perfect gentleman. Yet as sweet as it was, it was making her crazy. She wanted him. Her body was on fire. And she wasn't sure how long she could pretend that all she wanted on this Saturday evening was company and nice conversation. She closed her eyes and prayed for patience.

Spence opened the top of the grill, reached for a fork and stuck it deep into the steak. It was taking all his willpower to keep his fingers from peeling off Desiree's swimsuit and exposing that lush body to his eager eyes.

The desire to touch her, to explore every inch, every curve, to fill her body with his was making him stupid. He couldn't remember anything he'd said since she'd walked out onto the deck and dropped the sheer wrap to reveal what was underneath. He was pretty sure his mouth dropped open. He had to keep thinking about the most mundane things to keep his body under control. He'd kept a towel thrown over his lap to help disguise the erection that he was sure was hard enough to break concrete. And he'd dived into the pool, hoping to cool off in more ways than one. It had helped only for a little while.

He glanced over his shoulder. She was a work of art. His penis jumped to attention in total agreement. "Down, boy," he muttered. He closed the lid of the grill and headed for the water.

Desiree heard the splash and opened her eyes. She drew in a long breath, tossed her legs over the side of the chair and stood. She walked to the edge of the pool and dived in.

Spence emerged from under the water and saw her swimming toward him. They both bobbed in the water in the shallow end.

The hell with being a gentleman, he thought. His arm snaked around her waist and pulled her flush against him. He wanted her to feel his need, his want for her. His mouth covered hers and she was sweeter than he could have ever imagined. She moaned against his mouth and he cupped her round derriere, pulling her tight.

Desiree wrapped her arms around his neck and let

her tongue explore the heat of his mouth, thrilling in the way his tongue played with hers, sending ripples of desire scurrying along the length of her spine.

He pulled away and worshipped the line of her neck, planting tiny kisses on the soft skin down to the rise of her breasts, which played hide-and-seek above the water. He dared to ease one strap off her shoulder and then the other when he felt her shudder. He pushed the straps down and then the top of her suit until her full, luscious breasts were exposed. He cupped one in his hand, grazed her hard nipple with the tip of his fingers, and she sighed a ragged breath. Her eyelids fluttered. He lowered his head and took the nipple between his fingers and ran his tongue across it. Her body stiffened as if electrified.

"Spence…"

He paid homage to one and then the other and then back again, unable to get his fill of the taste of her, the feel of her flesh against his lips.

Desiree reached down into the water, felt for the waistband of his trunks and tugged at them until they were below his hips and his throbbing phallus was freed. She wrapped her hands around it and the sensation of feeling the length and width and power of him had her moaning his name and she slowly stroked him, feeling him pulse in her palm. She ran her thumb back and forth across the swollen head until he begged her to stop.

He held her wrist to put a momentary stop to the torture. "Not yet, baby," he whispered against the hollow of her neck. He pulled on her suit until it was down around her knees and she stepped out of it. Spence drew in a long, ragged breath as the reality of her totally naked body being his momentarily short-circuited his head. "I want you," he said before taking her mouth to hush the whimpers that rose when he toyed with her clit, which hardened and pulsed at his touch.

Spence slipped a finger inside of her and her body arched against him. Slowly, in and out, one, then two. He wanted her completely ready, open and needing him as badly as he needed her. Spence lifted her and she instinctively wrapped her legs around his waist.

She could feel the head of his penis pressing against her opening. She had to have him inside of her. She had to know what he felt like. She had to quench her thirst for him. She maneuvered her hand between their airtight bodies and grabbed him. She looked into his eyes, drew in a breath and pushed her hips forward.

Spence held her, rose up and pushed past her opening, spreading her. They both gasped at the surreal pleasure of that first contact. For a moment neither of them moved, needing to experience this moment for a little while longer.

The water lapped over them as Spence slowly moved in and out of her. She rested her head against his neck and closed her eyes as thrill after thrill rippled through her like the water that teased and embraced them.

Her eyes flew open when she realized that Spence was walking with her wrapped around him. He managed to get to the three steps that led to the deck and took them to dry land. He kissed her over and over again before easing them both down on the padded lounge chair with him still inside of her.

He tenderly wiped the water from her face, kissed her eyelids, stroked her hips, suckled her breasts.

She could feel his erection pulsing within her walls but nothing could have prepared her for his full and complete entry into her.

"Ooooooooh." Her cry of pleasure echoed into the encroaching night.

Spence pushed into Desiree again, deeper this time, longer. She trembled. Her fingers imprinted on his back. Slow and easy he pulled halfway out, then went back in. Her head swam.

He took her trembling thighs and draped them over his arms, eased out of her completely, and her nails dug into his skin when his head dipped down, his tongue trailing across her stomach. He pushed her legs farther back, wider apart, until her entire center was at his total mercy.

When his tongue laved her swollen clit, the only thing that kept them from being thrown to the ground when her body arched violently in response was the viselike grip that Spence had on her hips. He took her again and again, until every fiber of her being was on fire.

She stopped crying out. Her pleas for release were reduced to whimpers and shudders as her climax rose from the balls of her feet, up the back of her legs, in between her shaking thighs, straight up her center to the top of her head, only to cascade back down and explode in her center, which had her thrusting her pelvis against the heat of his mouth and his masterful tongue.

Desiree was limp, yet her body continued to jump and vibrate as if someone periodically touched her with a jolt of electricity. *Incredible,* was all she kept thinking over and over again. *Impossible* would follow. It was impossible for one person to make another person feel the way that Spence made her feel. But it couldn't be impossible, because he *had* made her feel that way. He took her body to someplace she had never been.

She held him as close as physics allowed. She needed to assure herself that he wasn't one of her many dreams about Spence. That he was real flesh and blood and that he'd just made love to her like she'd never been loved before.

The smell of smoke stirred them. Spence lifted his head from the pillow of her breasts.

"The steaks." He started to get up.

She pulled him back and cupped his face in her hands. "Put them out and then come up to my room. The last one at the end of the hallway."

The corner of his mouth curved upward. "Say no more."

Reluctantly he got up, kissed her and walked over to the grill.

Desiree sat up, then stood. Her breasts tingled. Between her legs still throbbed. She smiled with a kind of inner joy she couldn't remember ever feeling and headed for her room, determined to make Spence's mind spin the way he'd made hers spin.

Spence wrapped a towel around his waist, put out the grill and the cook in him shook his head at the ruined dinner. He stepped inside and closed and locked the glass sliding doors.

There was a part of him that still had a hard time processing what had finally happened between him and Desi. How long had he imagined the two of them together? How many women had he been with and wished were her, imagined that they were in order to get through the act?

Desiree was the woman he'd been waiting for, preparing himself for. Today was only the beginning. He intended to make her his own, for her to feel about him the way he felt about her.

He climbed the stairs, his heart thumping like that of a teen meeting his date for the first time. Her door was closed. He could see the flicker of light coming from underneath. He slowly opened the door and was greeted with soft candlelight and the heady scent of something woodsy and sexy. He closed the door and turned to his left. Desiree was seated in the middle of the bed, propped up against dozens of pillows, with a pale peach sheet pulled up just above the swell of her breast. Her curly hair was wild, her eyes bright, and her scent drew him to her like a moth to a flame.

As he came closer, she slowly pushed the sheet away. Her knees were bent and slightly parted, and he could just catch a glimpse of the dark paradise that rested between her thighs.

She put her right hand between her legs and cupped

her sex as if to hide it from him. The move was so sensuous, so erotic that Spence nearly came right where he stood.

His jaw clenched as he held on to his last ounce of willpower. Having to hold out while they were on the deck had him half out of his mind. He was so hard that it hurt and he wanted release, the kind that he knew Desiree would give him.

Her heart was pounding so loud, she knew that he could hear it. As bold and brazen as she might appear, she was shaking like a leaf inside. She wanted to satisfy him. She wanted him to remember this day for as long as time allowed, no matter what happened between them. She wanted to erase from his consciousness all the women who had come before her and brand his heart with her name…Desiree.

Spence sat beside her, leaned over and tenderly kissed her, so softly that her racing heart ached with joy. He stroked her cheek and his free hand covered hers at her center. He applied gentle pressure, massaged her palm and she trembled.

Desiree took her hand away and covered his, letting him do what he did best. She played with his fingers as they toyed with her, slipped in and out of her until she couldn't take it, and she held his hand in place, rocking her hips gently against his masterful touch.

"Desi," he whispered against her lips and stretched out beside her. He nuzzled her breast as she reached beneath her pillow and grasped the condom packet.

They'd been in her dresser for a while and she finally was going to use them. She handed it to him.

Spence tore the packet open with his teeth and rolled the condom on.

Desiree scampered to her knees and then straddled him. He gazed up at her.

"You are so beautiful," he said in awe as the candle-light played around the outline of her exquisite form.

She rose up on her knees until she was positioned directly above his stiff member. Slowly she eased herself down onto him and they both sucked in air as he filled her.

Chapter 16

Spence called the restaurant and advised Michelle that he would be out for the rest of the weekend and that she could reach him on his cell if there was an emergency. Thankfully, she didn't ask any questions and assured him that everything would be fine.

Since they'd arrived at their truce, things had not been quite the same between them. The ease that had been there was gone, but it had been replaced with a new acceptance of what could and could not be. He tucked his cell phone away and joined Desiree in the kitchen. They were both starving.

"Everything okay?" she asked while continuing to chop spinach for the salad.

"Yep. All is taken care of. How can I help?" he asked, easing up behind her and nuzzling the back of her neck.

She giggled and turned around into his arms. The top of her black silk robe slid open. "If you keep that up, we'll pass out from hunger," she teased, then kissed him lightly on the lips. "You can cut up that chicken on the counter."

"Yes, ma'am."

"Why did you decide to go into the restaurant business instead of cars?"

"I ask myself that all the time. It was really a toss-up, to be honest." He cut the roasted chicken down the middle and began slicing. "I suppose what tipped the scales was talking with your sister."

Desiree glanced at him over her shoulder, then went back to what she was doing. "Meaning?"

"She knew that I'd wanted my own business one day. I'd studied cooking and had spent years as an auto mechanic apprentice. She'd heard about the space that is now Bottoms Up and told me I should go for it. She put up some of the money."

Desiree stopped what she was doing. "She did?"

"Yeah. I thought you knew that."

"She never said a word."

"I'm surprised."

"So am I. Dom doesn't usually let a moment of her basking in the glow of her accomplishments go without trumpets."

They were quiet for a moment.

"So does that mean that she's part owner?" Desiree asked.

"No. I paid her back every dime with interest."

"Oh," she said pretty much to herself. "I guess you two really are close."

Spence put down the knife, wiped his hands on a towel and came up next to her. He took her chin between his two fingers, compelling her to meet his gaze. "Don't even go there. I promise you, there has never been anything, I mean nothing, between me and your sister... ever. It's not that kind of relationship." His eyes searched her face.

She pressed her lips together, then bobbed her head.

"You're the one I've been waiting for, Desi," he said softly. He brushed her curls away from her face. "The one I've been dreaming about."

She hooked her fingers into the loops on his jeans. "So have I." She leaned forward and lifted her head to meet his lips.

They spent the rest of the evening sipping wine, listening to music and telling each other stories from their childhood, what it was like growing up in a headline-making family and growing up with a single parent. School days and friendships, bad relationships and good ones. Before they realized it, the sun was peeking over the horizon and they finally went to bed, falling asleep to the beat of each other's heart.

When they awoke late the following morning, Spence said he needed to get home and take care of Howard and change clothes. Then maybe they could go for a drive or see a movie.

"You're coming with me," he said as he sat up and rubbed the sleep from his eyes.

Desiree stretched. Her body ached in new, pleasant ways. "I'm looking forward to meeting Howard."

"He'll love you. Just like I do."

Desiree froze. Her head snapped toward him. Her mouth tried to form words.

"Love me?"

"Yes. Love you, D. J. Lawson. I've been in love with you for so long, I can hardly remember a time when I wasn't," he admitted, and saying the words seemed to set him free. His soul opened up and he wanted to take her inside and show her exactly what he meant. "And it's not about sex, or the fact that you're a Lawson." He leaned toward her. "It's you. It's everything about you."

She scooted closer and fought back tears of joy. This was what she'd hoped for, prayed for. Spence Hampton, the man of her dreams, was in love with her.

"I've seen this day in my dreams a million times," she said, her voice shaking with emotion. "But I never thought it would come. And now it has." A tear slid down her cheek. "I was so determined to get you out of my system that I let my well-intentioned, if not crazy, sister talk me into seeing other men. But inside, I knew it would never work. It was you. It was always you that I was waiting for."

Spence wiped away the tear that hung at the corner of her mouth.

Desiree pulled the sheet away from her body. She ran her fingers down the center of his chest. Her eyes met his for a moment and then danced away. She turned onto her back and opened her arms and her body to him.

"I love you, too," she whispered an instant before he took her breath away.

* * *

When they arrived at Spence's house, Howard was waiting for them at the door. He leaped up on Spence, nearly knocking him down.

Spence rubbed him behind the ears. "I'm sorry, boy. But this lady here has my head all confused and I forgot to come home."

Howard barked in agreement.

"Howard, this is Desiree. You be nice to her."

"Hey, Howard. Hey, boy," she cooed and he hummed deep down in his throat and sniffed her hand.

"Told ya he was gonna love you. Come on in. Let me get him fed and take him for a walk." He led the way inside. "Make yourself comfortable."

Desiree followed him inside. His house was small and cozy, quite the opposite of the palatial accommodations she'd grown up in. The furnishings were totally male: warm chocolate leather seating, hardwood floors, blinds rather than drapes and the biggest flat-screen television she'd ever seen in her life. The low wooden table was covered in car and mechanics magazines. A stereo system took up another wall. She smiled to herself. This was so Spence.

"As soon as Howard is fed, I'll take him out," Spence said, reentering the living room. "In the meantime, I'll show you around. This," he said, spreading his arms, "is the living room. There's a small half bath just off the kitchen."

She walked behind him. He pushed open the swinging doors and the kitchen spread out before him. It was without a doubt a cook's kitchen. Stainless steel gleamed from the double-door refrigerator to the industrial oven, sink and dishwasher. One wall was filled with cookbooks, an open floor-to-ceiling cabinet held spices and condiments, the island had a built-in wok and burners, and wood cabinetry ran the expanse of the room. And it was spotless.

"This is incredible," she murmured, taking it all in.

"Other than my spot in front of the big screen, this is my favorite place in the house."

"So I see."

"I hope to fix many a meal for you here," he said, coming up to her and scooping her into his arms. He bent her over and took a long, leisurely kiss before letting her go. He took her hand. "Come on, I'll show you upstairs."

The second floor had a small room that he used for an office and a workout room, a full bath with a separate shower and the master bedroom. The king-size bed was the focal point and the warm browns were repeated. A beige-and-brown area rug set off the hardwood floors.

"Well, that's the grand tour," he said.

"I like it."

"Think you could be comfortable here?"

She smiled mischievously. "I know I could."

He walked over to his dresser and took out a change of underclothes. "Next time you come, I'll be sure to make some room for you in the dresser."

Her heart bumped in her chest. She couldn't wait to line up some of her lingerie next to his boxers.

* * *

The weekend went by much too quickly, and before they were ready, Spence was pulling up in front of Desiree's house.

"Are you coming in?"

"If I do, I can guarantee that neither one of us will get any sleep tonight." He kissed the tip of her nose. "You have a busy day tomorrow and so do I."

She caressed his face and he turned his mouth to kiss the inside of her palm.

They got out of the car and he walked with her up the steps. He took her keys and opened the front door. She stepped across the threshold, deactivated the alarm and then turned to him. Her heart swelled when she witnessed the warmth of desire in his eyes.

"It's going to be a long night without you, baby."

"Don't let it be," she responded.

"Go get your things. You're coming home with me." He shut the door behind them.

While Spence occupied himself down in the family room, Desiree was scurrying around her bedroom, tearing through her drawers and her closets, trying to find everything she needed. He did say he would make space for her in his dresser but he didn't say how much. Should she bring enough to hold her over for a while, or would that seem too presumptuous? She didn't want to scare him off. She grabbed a handful of bras and panties, two teddies, slippers, her toiletries, two dresses for work, a pair of jeans, sneakers and a T-shirt. She looked around, couldn't think of anything else and began packing her overnight bag. She put her dresses into a garment bag, shoved her netbook into her tote and she was ready.

When she came back downstairs, Spence was fully engaged in watching the Saints and the Jets.

"Who's winning?"

He barely glanced up. "Saints, seven to three."

Desiree shook her head and smiled, walked off to the kitchen, took a beer from the fridge, searched the pantry for some chips and pretzels and joined Spence on the couch. Sitting there with him, watching football on a Sunday evening, cheering and munching, with his arm draped around her shoulder, seemed like the most natural thing in the world.

By the time the game was over, it was after ten and they were both yawning and stretching. During the whole weekend that they'd been together, they'd probably slept six hours in total.

"Ready?" Spence said, lifting his brows to stretch his eyes.

"Yep. Let me put these things in the sink."

"I'll put your bag in the car."

"Wait. I'm just thinking, I'm going to need my car for tomorrow, so I'll follow you to your place."

He crossed the short distance between them. "I can drive you in the morning." He kissed her lightly on the lips. "Pick you up in the evening." He twirled her around in a smooth dance move. "And make love to you until the sun comes up."

"That offer is too tempting to turn down," she said over her laughter.

He winked. "I'll be out front."

"Right behind you."

While Spence put her overnight bag and tote in the trunk and her garment bag in the backseat, he considered a main reason why he didn't want to leave her alone, have her drive alone, come home alone. Max DeLaine had yet to be dealt with, and until he was, Spence was going to do everything that he could to keep Desiree under his watchful eye.

Just as Desiree was about to set the alarm, the house phone rang. She decided to let it just ring, but maybe it was her father.

She hurried down the hall and picked up the phone from the antique table in the foyer.

"Hello?"

"Hey, Desi, it's me."

"Dom…"

"Listen, I'm on my way home. Just landed."

"Oh, I thought you were coming back tomorrow."

"Yeah, so did I. But plans changed. Anyway, I should be there soon. I wanted to talk to you about the Platinum Society. I know I promised to back off, but I got a text from Melanie Harte and…"

"Dom…I know you have my best interests at heart but I won't be needing any dating service or any more help in finding a man."

"If this is still about Max, I swear I'll fix it."

"Dominique! Why won't you listen?"

"Desi!" Spence called out from the front door. "Come on, baby, it's getting later by the minute."

"Coming," Desiree called.

"Who was that? I'd swear it sounded like Spence." She laughed at the absurdity of that notion. Her sister and Spence! It would never happen.

For reasons that she couldn't explain, Desiree lied. "A friend. I'm going out. Won't be here when you get in. Be sure to set the alarm. Bye, Dom." She hung up before her sister could get in another word. Her heart was pounding. Why didn't she tell Dominique that Spence was waiting for her to join him in his car and take her to his home, where he was going to make love to her until the sun came up? Why didn't she tell her sister that Spence loved her, had always loved her, just as she'd always loved him?

She didn't. Somehow she couldn't. She palmed her house keys, set the alarm and walked to the door, where Spence was waiting.

"Everything okay?"

She looked up at him. "Yep. Let's go."

Yet all throughout the night, even as Spence worshipped every inch of her heated flesh, whispered over and over again how much he cared for her, the question taunted her. Why hadn't she told her sister?

Chapter 17

All day the staff at the city council kept commenting on how radiant and glowing Desiree looked. She'd gone in the restroom to look at her reflection, wondering if she could see what everyone else saw.

Her face looked the same. That wasn't it. It was what was going on inside that spilled onto her expression, her body language. She was bubbling inside, bubbling over with happiness. During the day she found herself staring at nothing and more than once Valerie asked her what in the world she was smiling about.

By the time Patrice called and asked if she wanted to do lunch, she was ready to burst. "Girl, I have so much to tell you."

They met at their favorite little bistro just off of King Charles Avenue. They decided to eat outside and take in the beautiful afternoon.

"Don't you dare leave out one detail," Patrice warned. "I've been going crazy waiting to hear what happened."

The waitress came and took their orders, and the moment she was out of earshot, Desiree launched into her account of her jaw-dropping weekend with Spence.

Patrice ooh-weed and oh, girl'd, the entire conversation. By the time Desiree was finished relaying the tamer parts of her weekend, Patrice was fanning herself. "All night, Desi?"

"All night, girl. The man is—what can I say?—incredible." Her gaze drifted off as she relived when they were standing up against the wall in his bedroom or in the chair by the window, with nothing covering them but the light from the moon.

Patrice snapped her fingers in front of Desiree's face. "Earth to Desiree."

Desiree blinked. "Sorry."

"All I can say is, it's about damned time." She slapped her palm on the table. "I told you to just go for it, didn't I?"

"Yeah, yeah, you did."

"You took things over to his place?"

Desiree nodded, which reminded her of Dominique's call. She hadn't seen her sister since she'd come home and she hadn't returned the several messages that Dominique left on her cell phone. She was still struggling with why she was keeping her relationship with Spence a secret from her sister when what she wanted to do was shout it out to the world.

"So what does Dominique have to say?" Patrice asked before biting into her panini.

"I haven't told her."

Patrice put down her sandwich and wiped her mouth with the paper napkin. "Why?"

Desiree puffed her cheeks and shook her head. "I don't know," she said on a breath.

"She should be happy for you." Patrice waited, watching the look of doubt and anxiety play across Desiree's face.

"Yeah, she should."

"So what is it, then? I know it's not because you think there was something going on with them."

Desiree shook her head. "Not...physically. I don't know how to explain it. It's just a feeling I have. I know my sister. She's not going to take it well."

Patrice lifted her glass of lemon-flavored water to her lips. "You can't keep it a secret. So you may as well make up your mind and tell her. Dominique is a big girl with a life of her own. Whatever her issues may or may not be, she'll get over it." She took a long swallow of water and put her glass down. "Just tell her."

Desiree stabbed the piece of salmon in her salad. "I will."

For the rest of the afternoon, between phones calls, an office meeting, paperwork, brief whispered sexy chats with Spence, Desiree thought about what she would say to Dominique. Spence planned on picking her up after work as promised but he said that he had to go back to the restaurant until closing.

Spence arrived at her office at the appointed time and Desiree climbed in his car. "Do you want to come back to my place tonight? I can swing by and pick you up when I'm done at the restaurant. Or I can take you there now. You can relax and unwind. You do have some of your things there."

He smiled at her and her insides tingled at the prospect. But reality stepped in. She fastened her seat belt. "I really need to go home. I have some things to take care of."

He turned the key in the ignition. "Not a problem. I'll come and get you after I close up."

She settled back in her seat and hoped that things would go smoothly with Dominique.

"I know you said you would think about it, but what have you decided about DeLaine?" he asked as they turned the corner onto her street.

Her stomach tightened. She gave a short shake of her head. "I just want to forget about it. I don't think he's going to be bothering me again. Not after the other day."

"Maybe not, Desi. But he's still out there and maybe a threat to some other woman who doesn't have someone to look out for her."

She turned and looked at him and the firm set of his jaw and the concern in his eyes had her rethinking her stance. She didn't believe deep down inside that Max was actually dangerous, but it wasn't up to her to decide. She needed to file a complaint, at least get it on file.

"I'll talk to my brother-in-law, Preston, and find out

if and how I can file a complaint and hopefully keep our family name out of it."

"Promise?"

She nodded. "Promise."

"Good. I'll feel a lot better when you have that taken care of." He pulled into the driveway and shut off the engine. "Lights are on." He opened his door and came around to her side and opened hers. "Guess Dominique is home."

"It's probably Justin," she said a bit too quickly.

"Hmm." He shrugged. "Her car is here. I should come in and say hello."

Her throat went dry.

His cell phone rang. He pulled it from his shirt pocket and looked at the number on the face. "It's the restaurant. Excuse me a sec," he said to Desiree. He pressed Talk. "Hey, Nichole, what's up?… No, absolutely not."

Desiree thought this was her perfect opportunity. She kissed his cheek and mimed that she would call him. Deep in his conversation with Nichole he nodded in agreement and got back in the car. "Hang on a minute, Nikki. Desi, I'll be back for you around eleven," he said before he shut the door and backed out of the driveway.

The moment Desiree put her key in the door, Dominique pulled it open. She stood in the doorway, looked at her sister and at the car she knew better than her own that was pulling away.

"I thought I heard voices. What was Spence doing here and why didn't he come in?"

Desiree stepped around her sister and walked inside.

She tossed her keys into the crystal bowl on the foyer table and went into the kitchen.

Dominique trailed behind her. "What's with you, anyway? I called you today but you didn't return my calls. You practically hung up on me last night. If you're still pissed off, I said I was sorry," she said, her voice rising. "How many times do you want me to say it?"

Desiree spun toward her. "I'm seeing Spence."

Dominique jerked back as if she'd been hit. She shook her head. "What? Seeing Spence?" She sputtered a laugh. "What are you talking about?"

"We're seeing each other, Dom. It was Spence's voice you heard last night."

Dominique frowned as if she could squeeze some sense into the nonsense her sister was saying. She stared at her reflection that looked back at her and waited for Desiree to say that she was kidding. But she didn't. Dominique started to laugh and couldn't stop. She laughed until tears spilled from her eyes.

"Spence and you! Hilarious." She wiped her eyes. "Whew." She blew out a breath and leaned her hip against the counter. "Okay, the joke is over. You made me laugh." She hopped up on the bar stool beneath the island.

Desiree pulled out a stool and sat opposite Dominique. "Why is it so impossible for you to believe that Spence and I could be together?" she asked, trying to control the hurt that shook her voice.

Dominique's gaze ran over her sister's face. Desiree's unflinching expression was one she was very familiar with—pure sincerity. "You're serious."

Desiree slowly nodded her head. "And I've never been happier, Dom. I can't tell you how long I've thought about, cared about, wanted Spence," she said, her voice taking on an almost breathless note.

Dominique pushed back from the counter and stood. She ran her fingers through her short pixie hairstyle. "You…you don't know what you're getting into. You don't know Spence. I do." She banged a finger against her chest. "He's a playboy. He'd eat you alive and you wouldn't know what happened." Her voice was rising to near hysteria. "You don't know anything about men like Spence."

"Why are you doing this?" Desiree yelled. "Why can't you be happy for me? This is what you wanted." She threw her hands up in the air. "For me to have the perfect man. Well, I do."

Dominique vigorously shook her head. "No. He's not perfect. He'll break your heart. Don't say I didn't warn you," she said and stormed out, leaving Desiree stunned, shaken and angry.

She'd been hesitant to tell Dominique only because she felt that Dominique might have feelings for Spence, even if she'd never acted on them. But she'd never expected the over-the-top outrage. She recalled the way her sister demeaned her, basically telling her that she couldn't compete on any level with other women, especially when it came to Spence. She'd hoped that Dominique would be happy for her. Her heart ached. She and Dominique had had their arguments in the past. All sisters did. This was different. This was intentionally hurtful. A hurt that she didn't deserve.

Above her a door slammed; then she heard footsteps pounding down the steps. Moments later the front door opened and slammed shut.

Desiree flinched. She closed her eyes and drew in a long, deep breath. Dominique would have to deal with her temper tantrum. She was going to lie down for a while and wait to hear from Spence. She got up from the stool, switched off the lights and went upstairs.

She stripped out of her clothes, separated what needed to go in the laundry and what needed dry cleaning, snatched up her robe from the foot of her bed and headed for the shower.

Chapter 18

Dominique was so hurt, so furious, she could barely see through her tears. How could they do this to her? How? She sped down the darkened streets, not knowing where she was going, only knowing that she needed to get away. She drove around for nearly half an hour before she turned around and headed toward Spence's restaurant.

She screeched into a parking space and jumped out of the car and went storming into the restaurant. She marched right up to the reception podium.

"Ms. Lawson," Nichole greeted, full of cheer. "Are you staying for dinner?"

"Can you please let Spence know that I'm here?" she snapped. She folded her arms and tapped her foot to keep from coming apart.

"Sure." Nichole picked up the house phone and

pressed the number for Spence's office. "Um, hi… Ms. Lawson is here to see you. I'll send her right back." Nichole hung up the phone. "He's in his office. He said to—"

Before Nichole could finish her sentence, Dominique had brushed by her and was heading through the restaurant to the back. She pushed through the doors that led to the tiny offices and kept going until she reached Spence's door. She pushed it open and she could tell by the startled look on his face that she was not the Lawson that he was expecting.

"Dom." He frowned in confusion, stood and came around his desk. "What are you doing here?" He came up to her to kiss her cheek and she stepped out of his reach. "What is it?" He clasped her shoulders and looked into her eyes and realized that she'd been crying. "Baby, what happened? Why are you crying?"

She tugged away. "Don't act like you give a damn, Spence, because you don't!"

"What? What is wrong with you?"

"My sister, Spence. You and my sister! How could you?"

For a moment he was too stunned to put words together. He shook his head to clear it. "Let me get this straight. You come charging in here like a U.S. marshal because you have some kind of issue about me seeing your sister? You have got to be kidding me, Dom."

"Do I look like I'm joking? Does it sound like I'm joking? What are you doing with her? She's not your type."

"My type. How do you know who my type is?"

"Because I know you, that's why! I know you better than you know yourself. You're only going after her because that's what you do, go after women and then drop them." She was so furious she was shaking.

"That's what you think of me? That I'm some kind of dog that spends all their time sniffing around women? You think you know me, Dominique, but you don't know anything about me."

"She's not the woman for you. She's not."

"You can't run my life, Dominique." He whirled away from her, afraid of where his temper was taking him. "I have my own life. A life that doesn't always include you or need your approval." He ran his hand across his close-cut hair.

"How can you say that?" Her voice cracked. Tears streamed freely down her cheeks. "I love you. Don't you get it?" With that she stormed out, nearly knocking Michelle over.

Spence was rooted to the spot, held in place by Dominique's emotional confession until Michelle stuck her head in. "You okay? I heard the yelling all the way in the wine cellar."

"Yeah, yeah." He rushed by her. "Sorry," he said on his way out.

Michelle watched him and wondered for the zillionth time what was so special about those Lawson sisters.

Spence rushed through the dining area, offering the barest of greetings to some of his guests as he headed for the front door. After what seemed like forever he reached the door and pushed through it. He ran out onto the sidewalk and looked left and right, just as Dominique's Benz turned the corner.

He bent over, rested his hands on his knees, then stood and turned in a slow circle of frustration. After a few moments he went back inside. He had to call Dominique. He couldn't leave things like this between them. In love with him! Damn it.

Spence went back to his office and shut the door. He dialed Dominique's cell. The phone rang and rang and went to her voice mail. He hung up, waited a few minutes and called back. He tried several more times, until she finally answered.

"Where are you?"

"What do you care?"

"You know I care, Dom. We need to talk."

"No, we don't." She disconnected the call.

He slammed his fist down on the desk and muttered a string of curses. "Fine." He pushed back from his desk and grabbed his jacket from the coatrack near the door. He found Michelle.

"I'm done for the night. See you in the morning."

"Sure. Anything I can do, Spence?"

He looked at her, saw the real question behind her eyes. He squeezed her hand. "Thanks for asking. I'll work it out."

Spence stepped out in the cool evening. He put on his jacket. On any other night, especially a night like the one he was having, he would take the Mustang out for a drive and try to clear his head. Instead he walked to his Lexus and got behind the wheel. For a few minutes he simply sat there, thinking, or at least trying to.

Dominique was always out there. High-strung and dramatic. But this was a bit much even for her. In his wildest dreams he would have never thought that Dominique would say those things about him, about her sister, and then say that she was in love with him. He shook his head.

He'd give Dominique some time to cool off and then try to talk to her. He took out his cell phone and dialed Desiree. He hoped that Dominique hadn't stormed back home to take her frustrations out on her sister.

Desiree's cell phone rang and rang. The voice mail came on. He left a short message, then dialed the house phone. No answer. A knot began to build in his stomach. He tried her cell again, even as he turned the key in the ignition and put the car in gear.

He kept her number on redial as he barely stayed under the speed limit on his way to her house. With each passing minute, his anxiety grew.

Desiree stood near her dresser, clutching her robe in her fist. When she'd stepped out of the bathroom, he was there, sitting in her room. She screamed but she knew no one would hear her.

"We're all alone," Max said.

"How…how did you get in here?" She backed away from him.

He smiled but it didn't reach his eyes, which looked distant and detached. "The door was open. I saw Dominique when she went tearing out of here. We actually drove past each other on the street. She didn't even see me." He shook his head, as if that was totally beyond his comprehension.

Desiree swallowed. Her throat was bone-dry. "What do you want, Max?"

"I told you. I only wanted to talk. Sit down so that we can talk," he said, pointing to the bed.

Her legs were so weak she felt sure she would collapse before she got to the other side of the room and her bed. She tightened the belt on her robe and eased down onto the mattress.

Her cell phone rang. Her heart banged in her chest. She knew it was probably Spence. Then the house phone rang, then her cell again. It all made Max that much more incensed.

"Stop the ringing!"

"I should answer. Then whoever it is will stop calling."

He laughed. "Why wouldn't you go out with me again? I would have treated you nice. Opened doors, picked up the check. Isn't that the kind of man you were looking for?"

She didn't know what the right answer was. No matter what she said, it wouldn't matter. She could tell by the dazed look in his eyes that he didn't care what she said, and that realization was more frightening than anything else.

"I always treat women well, but…" His voice drifted off. Then he focused on Desiree again. "Some of them never want a second date." He looked at her. "Why do you think they don't want to see me again?"

Desiree tightened her hold on her robe.

* * *

Spence pulled into the driveway and noticed the car parked there. It wasn't Dominique's Benz or Desiree's Volvo. He got out of the car and went to the front door. It was partially ajar. He eased it open all the way. The downstairs was in total darkness, but he heard voices from upstairs.

"I don't know!" he heard Desiree shout. The hair on the back of his neck stood up.

He took out his phone and dialed 911. He quickly and in a hush relayed the information. There was an intruder, he said, at the Lawson mansion. He was on the second floor. Someone needed to come immediately.

Spence disconnected the call and eased down the hallway and slowly inched up the steps. The voices drew closer, became clearer. He cleared the top of the landing. The light was on in Desiree's room.

"All you had to do was let me take you out again. That wasn't too much to ask! Was it?"

"No," Desiree responded.

"That's all I needed to hear you say."

Spence reached the door. Max had his back turned to him but must have sensed him. He swung toward the door. Spence held up his hands.

"We're going to do this easy. I want you to let Desiree come to me."

Max shook his head. "We have to have our second date first. She promised me."

"Desi…" Spence slowly entered the room, careful not to make any sudden moves. Nothing to spook him. He had no idea what Max was capable of and he wasn't taking any chances. He eased along the side of the room, trying to get between Max and Desiree.

The red-and-white flashing lights of the police car shone through the window. Max looked around, startled and uncertain.

In that short window of indecision Spence got to Desiree and gathered her up in his arms just as four officers burst into the room.

Desiree buried her face in Spence's chest, while Max continued yelling that he only wanted to talk.

After Max had been handcuffed, read his rights and taken away, Desiree spent the next half hour giving a report to one of the responding officers. He said he'd be in touch if he had any more questions.

Spence locked up behind them, then turned to Desiree.

"Either I'm staying here or you're coming to my place. Your choice. But I'm not leaving you alone." He didn't even want to think about what could have happened or what was really on Max's twisted mind.

Desiree nodded. "I'll get dressed."

He went with her upstairs. There was no way that he was letting her out of his sight.

"How did he get in here?" he asked, collapsing in the side chair while Desiree got dressed.

"Apparently when Dom stormed out of here earlier, she didn't lock the door behind her. He just walked right in." A shiver ran through her.

"Seems like Dominique is on a real roll tonight," he said, more to himself.

"Huh?"

"Nothing. What was she upset about?"

Desiree drew in a deep breath. "I told her about you and me and she…flipped." She waved her hand. "I don't understand it and I really don't want to talk about Dominique right now."

He pressed his lips together and nodded. He didn't want to talk about Dominique, either.

She picked up her purse from the top of the dresser. "I'm ready."

Spence got up, came over to her, took her in his arms and held her. Held her as if he never wanted to let her go. She clung to him, fighting back the tears that she'd held at bay for the past two hours, and the magnitude of what she'd experienced suddenly came crashing down on her. Her sobs shook her petite frame.

Spence stroked her back. "It's all right. It's over now," he whispered against her hair. "I'm here. I'm here."

Chapter 19

Before Desiree went with Spence, she left a long message for Dominique about what had happened and a similar message for Rafe on their voice mails. She advised them both that she was staying with Spence and they could reach her there.

Starlight filtered into the bedroom. "I should have listened to you," Desiree said as she snuggled against the cocoon of Spence's arms.

He stroked the curve of her bare back. "It's behind us now. Max is where he belongs."

"How could he have fit in so well and been so crazy?"

"I wish I knew. I'm sure someone will enjoy trying to figure it out." He kissed the top of her head. "The only thing that's important is that you're safe. You're here with me, and I'm not going to let anything ever happen to you."

She angled her head to try and look at him. "You do have that knight-in-shining-armor appeal about you," she said softly and pressed her lips to his.

"We all have our skills, baby," he said and gently turned her on her back.

She draped one leg around his thigh. "And some of our skills are better than others."

The following morning, Desiree called her office and let them know that she would be out for the day. By the time she hung up, she had two messages on her phone. One from Dominique and the other from Rafe. Rafe was actually out of town, visiting friends in Sag Harbor, and said that as long as that bastard was off the street, he felt comfortable waiting until the next day to come back, and reminded her that she should have let him take care of the SOB when he'd started to. He added that he couldn't be happier about her and Spence, and when he came home, they would have to go out and celebrate.

Dominique's call, of course, was filled with drama and tears. She kept saying over and over that she had no idea about Max and how sorry she was about everything. She had spent the night at Zoie's house and would be home later and she hoped that Desiree would find it in her heart to forgive her.

Spence set a cup of freshly brewed coffee in front of her. Howard came and sat at her feet. She rubbed the top of his head.

"Everything cool?" He sat down and sipped his coffee.

She told him about the messages.

"At least your family knows what's going on."

"The officer that took the report last night said that he would keep it low-key. I'm hoping he keeps his word. I really don't think I could deal with a media feeding." She sighed heavily. "Still have to call Daddy and Lee Ann and Justin."

He took her hand. "Don't worry about all of that right now. Take the morning to regroup. I have to go to the restaurant for a couple of hours. When I get back, I'll be here with you when you make those calls. Okay?"

"Thanks."

He got up. "Howard will keep you company until I get back."

"Hear that, Howard?"

He barked in response.

"I'll be back before you know it." He leaned over, drew her to him and kissed her slow and sweet. "See you in a couple of hours." He grabbed his car keys and headed out.

Desiree wandered into the living room, curled up on the couch and turned on the mammoth television. She flipped through the channels, looking for any hint that the media had gotten wind of the story. But she was pretty sure that Max DeLaine's father didn't want the news of his son's arrest all over the television and in the papers, either. She finally settled on an old black-and-white romance movie, but before she knew it, she felt her eyes closing and she wouldn't have been able to tell a soul what the movie was about.

Spence's intention was to get in and out of the restaurant as quickly as possible. Even with that creep behind bars, he was still uneasy about leaving Desiree alone. Just thinking about how very wrong things could have gone last night had him wound up tighter than a guitar string.

He breezed through the now closed dining room and went straight back to the kitchen. His full staff was already at their stations in preparation for the lunch crowd.

"Hey, boss," Steven greeted.

"How's everything going?"

"We're all set up for the day. Just a couple of deliveries and we're good. Waiting on a vegetable delivery now. I'm pretty sure Michelle has that all taken care of, though."

"I made a few adjustments to the menu."

Steven nodded. "We have it covered. So if you need to go…" He let the statement hang in the air.

"I'm gonna take care of a few things and I'm out."

"Good." He clapped Spence on the back. "You deserve some time off. You work your ass off for this place. Relax. We can handle it."

"Thanks, Steven. I appreciate that." He started to walk off, stopped and turned back. "But if you need me, you know how to reach me."

Steven smiled indulgently. "Sure do, boss."

Spence walked out the kitchen's back exit and down the dark, narrow hallway to his office.

He unlocked his office door and shut it behind him. He wanted to take a quick look at the inventory list and make a few calls to confirm the entertainment for the upcoming week.

Just as he was about to pick up the phone, the tapping on the door drew his attention.

"Come in."

"Hey. I wasn't expecting you today." Michelle stepped into his office, looking as picture-perfect as always.

After what happened last night, he'd been having some real tugs of conscience himself about him and Michelle. That, too, could have taken a very bad turn. He was thankful that it had worked out and that they were both mature enough to accept what could and could not happen between them.

"Not here for long. I wanted to check a few things, make some calls."

She leaned against the door frame. "Everything cool?"

"Yeah."

She glanced down, then looked across the room at him. "So you're seeing one of the Lawson sisters?"

He cleared his throat.

"Which one?"

"Desiree."

She gave a short laugh. "I always thought it would be the other one." She drew in a breath. "I'm happy for you. As long as you're happy. Seriously."

"Thanks. I appreciate that."

"Well…" She brushed her hands down the length of her dress. "I better get busy. When do you think you'll be back?"

"Couple of days. By the weekend for sure."

She nodded and turned to leave, then stopped. "Did you hear on the news that Max DeLaine was arrested last night?"

"What?"

"Yeah, something about breaking and entering. It was real sketchy. I'm pretty sure his father is putting the lid on that story as we speak."

"Did it mention whose house was broken into?"

"No." She shook her head. "He seemed like a really nice guy."

"You've met him?"

"Yeah. A few times. He even asked me out but…" She shrugged and frowned slightly. "Not really sure why but the date never happened. Can't remember. It was a while ago." She focused on Spence. "Glad I didn't."

"Yeah.

"Anyway, let me get to work. I'll call you if anything comes up." She walked out.

So it wasn't being kept quiet. And if DeLaine Sr.'s arms weren't long enough to reach into all the nooks and crannies, it would be no time before the full story was all over the news, which was the last thing that Desiree wanted.

He got up, grabbed his keys, switched off the lights and locked up. If this thing broke, he didn't want Desiree to be by herself.

When he stepped outside with the intention of

walking to his car, a midnight-blue Mercedes-Benz pulled up in front of him. Dominique got out.

"Spence…"

She looked so lost and vulnerable that for a moment, he almost forgot that this fiasco was partly her fault, not to mention the things she'd said to her sister and her confession to him.

He slung his hands into the pockets of his jeans. "Dom."

She tentatively approached him. "Can we talk?"

"I tried to do that but you weren't listening."

"I know. I know. I've been…a bitch." Her lips pinched into a tight line. "I should have never said what I did. And I'm sorry."

"About what part?"

"All of it. I said some really crazy and thoughtless things."

"Let's go over there and sit down," he said, stretching his hand toward a bench beneath the tree.

They crossed the street and sat down. Dominique studied her hands as if the lines in the palms of her hands held the words that she needed to speak.

"I was being selfish and spoiled," she finally admitted. "There was this silly, greedy part of me that only wanted you for myself. You're my best friend, Spence, closer to me than anyone. You know me better than anyone, and when you get involved with someone…it takes away from us. I felt like I was going to lose you." She drew in a long breath, then looked directly at him. "I do love you. I've always loved you. But it wasn't until this morning, after all the dust had settled, that I realized it wasn't the kind of love to build a life on. I love you as my friend. Like my brother. And my sister's happiness is more important to me than anything." She wiped the tears away from her eyes. "Even if she doesn't believe it."

He put his arm around her shoulder and rested his head on top of hers. "She believes it." He squeezed her shoulder. "If you're not busy, I can prove it to you."

She looked up at him. "What do you mean?"

"Hop in your car and follow me."

Fifteen minutes later they were parking in front of Spence's town house.

Dominique locked the car and followed Spence up the path to the front door.

"What is going on?"

"I'm giving you your chance to make your sister believe you." He turned the key and opened the door. He heard the hum of the television coming from the living room. They went in that direction.

Desiree turned her head at their approach. Her eyes widened in surprise when she saw her sister. But they all focused on the screen as they listened to the news anchor relay the events of the previous night, mentioning that the victim of the alleged breaking and entering was none other than Senator Branford Lawson's daughter Desiree, head of the local city council.

Desiree covered her face with her hands and shook her head in misery.

Dominique groaned and plopped down in the first available seat.

"There is no clear explanation for the behavior of Max DeLaine," the reporter was saying, "but there is speculation that this may have been a romance gone bad."

"What!" Desiree leaped up from her seat. She began to pace. Spence intercepted her on her third pass across the floor.

"Take it easy. We'll figure this out. It was almost impossible that this whole mess could be kept quiet. Not with a name like his and yours in the picture."

Desiree's shoulders slumped. She sat down. "One thing that Daddy always taught us when it came to the media and to potential scandal was to stay ahead of the game. Right now, we're a step behind," she said, easily slipping into the role for which she'd been groomed since she was a little girl.

"Maybe we should call Lee Ann," Dominique meekly offered. "She's the political strategist. She'll know what to do."

Desiree turned her full attention on her sister. "And so do I."

Chapter 20

Desiree had made it a practice to keep a generally low profile, especially in her adult life. She didn't pose for pictures and she rarely, if ever, used her name or her connections to get what she wanted. It had always been her desire to achieve her goals on her own terms. Today was different. Today she intended to use the full weight of the Lawson name and all the powers of persuasion that she'd been mastering over the years.

Within a matter of two hours, she had strategically contacted selected print outlets, sent for Valerie from her office to help with the calls, set up "headquarters" in Spence's living room, arranged for a televised press conference on the front lawn of the Lawson mansion at four o'clock, prepared her remarks and worked on a press release with Valerie.

Spence watched in awe and with a chest full of pride

as he witnessed her work her show, never hesitating, never missing a beat and getting exactly what she wanted each and every time.

A part of him admired what she was doing and another part of him was uneasy. It was hard to admit that he could never do for her what she could do for herself. With one phone call her name and legacy could move mountains. She was confident and in charge, and the focused, almost hard-edged look that hovered in her eyes while she wrapped those reporters around her finger unnerved him.

He wanted to make a life with Desiree. It was what he'd been looking forward to for years. But if he did, would he become Mr. Lawson? The prince to the queen? He smiled, but then again, what could he expect from a woman who secretly raced cars on the weekend?

"Hey," she said softly, snapping him out of his reverie. She was kneeling down in front of him.

He blinked and focused on her. A smile moved across his mouth and his chest filled when he looked into her eyes and saw what was really in her heart. And it didn't matter if he was Mr. Lawson or the senator's daughter's husband as long as he had Desiree.

He stroked her cheek. "Taking a breather?"

"Yeah, everything is in place." She took his hand and kissed the inside of his palm. "I'm sorry to turn your place into public relations central. But I knew my office at the city council and my house were both out of the question. The reporters are already camped out there. I'd never get anything done."

"Don't worry about it. You do what you have to do.

Mi casa es su casa." He grinned. "Quite frankly, I'm impressed. I've never seen this side of you."

She ducked her head. "I guess I'm doing okay. I got a call from my father, who, short of giving me an outright compliment, said that he'd gotten wind that I was a force to be reckoned with."

He lifted her chin with the tip of his finger and kissed her forehead. He stood and pulled her to her feet. "Let's find someplace where we can talk."

They walked through the kitchen and out to the small enclosed porch. Spence sat on the bench and patted the space beside him. He put his arm around her shoulder and pulled her close.

"I know you have a lot going on right now. But I want to clear the air." He told her about Dominique's visit and her confession of love and her subsequent retraction of sorts. That she only wanted her to be happy. "I know that you and Dom have a lot of unspoken issues between you. I'm hoping that when the dust really settles, the two of you can work things out."

She rested her head on Spence's shoulder. "We will. We have to. It's long overdue."

"Ready?" Dominique asked as she peeked out of the window at the lawn covered with reporters, cameras and lights.

Desiree took a final look at her reflection in the hall mirror. Valerie handed her the statement that they'd prepared. She drew in a long breath. This would be her first press conference where she was the actual speaker and focus. For a moment she didn't think she could do it. But she thought about her mother, Louisa, and all the training she'd instilled in them as children. As well as the years of watching her father and the political "aunts and uncles" that were always a part of her life and, of course, her sister Lee Ann, who taught her everything she knew.

"Yes, I'm ready."

Valerie opened the door and Desiree stepped out to an explosion of flashbulbs and a surge of questions.

Desiree stepped up to the podium that had been set up and placed her remarks on the smooth surface. She surveyed the crowd until she spotted Spence, and the knots in her stomach began to loosen.

"Thank you all for coming. The reason for this press conference is to bring awareness to women across the state of Louisiana and the country. Never step back from reporting a crime. Never feel that it would be better to leave things alone. That's what I did. When Max DeLaine showed up at my office, then at my home the first time, I should have reported it then. I didn't. And last night this same man entered my home." She took a breath. "I could have stopped him before last night but I didn't. I was worried that reporting him would embarrass his family and stir up problems for mine. But I could have been a statistic. So I say this to women everywhere. Don't let fear or embarrassment steal your voice. You need to be heard." She paused. "Thank you all for coming." She turned and walked proudly back inside, even as a barrage of questions trailed her.

Seated around the backyard pool, Rafe, Justin, Dominique, Desiree and Spence discussed the events of the past few weeks. Dominique profusely apologized again for all her monumental screwups. News of Max DeLaine was finally off of the front page of the paper. Rafe admitted that he was actually seeing someone that he was really interested in. She lived in Sag Harbor and he planned on bringing her down to meet the family later in the year. All eyes widened at that confession. Justin was ready to take his bar exam, which they all toasted.

Desiree saved her news for last. "I got a call this morning from Uncle Jerry." Better known to the rest of the world as Congressman Jeremiah Davis, Branford's oldest and dearest friend and godfather to the entire Lawson clan.

"What's old Uncle Jerry up to?" Rafe asked before taking a sip from his glass of bourbon.

Desiree looked to Spence, who gave her a nod of reassurance. "There's a position available in Washington, on a committee that deals with women's rights." She swallowed. "He thinks I would be perfect to head up that committee and it would give me entrée to the national stage."

Dominique leaned forward, blinking in disbelief. "And?"

"I have a couple of weeks to decide."

"What's to decide, Cher?" Rafe said. "It's what you've been groomed for. The city council is a small stepping stone and Capitol Hill is a bigger one." He finished off his drink and pointed his glass at her. "You need to take it. What do you think, Spence?"

All eyes turned in his direction. When she'd talked

with him about it earlier, his initial response had been no. Why would she want to leave Louisiana? Why would she want to leave him when they'd just found each other? But then he'd realized that it wasn't up to him to pave the way for her life. If he intended to be a part of it, then he wanted to make sure that he supported her decisions, allowed her to grow, take on challenges and be all the woman that she could be. That was the woman he fell in love with. The enticing, smart, sexy, layered woman who had the whole world in front of her. Desiree Lawson was destined for something great, something bigger than Baton Rouge, and he wanted to make sure that she got it.

He looked at Desiree, a smile of pride on his lips. "I figure if this little fireball can get behind the wheel of a Ferrari and tear around a track at one hundred thirty miles an hour, she can damn near do whatever she wants."

Desiree covered her face and hid her shock at being outed and laughed at the expressions on their faces, while Dominique and Justin virtually pounced on her with questions and demands for explanations.

Rafe, of course, sat back, shook his head and laughed. He raised his glass to her and winked.

"Do you really think I should take this job in Washington?" Desiree asked as she sat in bed next to Spence.

He adjusted the pillow behind his head. "Do I want you to leave Baton Rouge? Of course not. Especially now. Maybe if we'd had more time…to build a strong foundation. That's the ideal situation—you live here forever, marry me and I take care of you." He glanced at her. "But I'm also a realist. You need to do this. You need to do this, the same way you need to race that car, the same way you need to run the city council, the same way you need to help people, to right wrongs. It's who you are." He turned on his side. "I would never think of stopping that, of stopping you. If you stayed here and we created this postcard relationship, you'd hate me for it one day."

A knot built in her throat. "So what are you saying? That we can't make it work? Lee Ann and Preston worked out their long-distance relationship. We can, too." She knew she was beginning to sound desperate, but she couldn't help it. Suddenly everything seemed to be falling apart.

"Baby, this is your time. I want you to take this opportunity and go for it." He covered her body with his.

"What about us?"

He kissed her lips and tried not to think about being unable to kiss her, to make love to her. He parted her thighs with a sweep of his leg. He planted hot kisses along her neck, moved down to caress her breasts with the heat of his tongue. Her moan filled him, soothed his soul. And when he entered her and she cried out his name, gripped him deep inside of her, with every downward stroke, every thrust, every groan that rose from the center of his being, he wanted her to know his love, and that it would always be there for her.

Chapter 21

Desiree had been in Washington for almost a month and it had been an endless array of nonstop activity. Setting up the committee, it turned out, was her role and responsibility. The majority of her day was spent on the phone and in meetings. She came home to her small newly rented apartment exhausted but energized. She believed in what she was doing and knew that she could make a difference.

Having her sister Lee Ann and her brother-in-law, Preston, nearby helped to ease the pangs of home-sickness. But as was typical of her father, even though they were in the same town, she rarely saw him.

But nothing could ease the pangs of not seeing and being with Spence. They talked most every night and they'd even seen each other over a weekend since she'd been gone. It wasn't enough and the ache inside her continued to grow. There were many lonely nights in which the emptiness grew so profound that she wanted to pack up and go home.

She couldn't. She'd made a commitment and she intended to keep it—somehow.

"You've been walking around here like a ghost for weeks," Michelle said to Spence while they went over the wine order.

"Hmm."

She put down her clipboard and sat on one of the wooden benches in the basement. "You're in love with her."

His eyes jerked toward Michelle.

"And you miss her and it's affecting your objectivity and your productivity. Instead of you being an asset around here lately, we're all tripping over you or trying to stay out of your way. Your head obviously is not here."

"I don't know what you're talking about."

"Don't be dense. You know perfectly well what I'm talking about." She reached across the space and took his hands in hers. "Look at me for a minute. We've been friends for a long time…more than friends over the years. I know how much you want to hold on to the reins but maybe it's time to let go."

His eyes flashed. "What are you saying?"

"I'm saying maybe it's time for you to go after *your* dream."

* * *

Desiree was bone tired by the time she put her key in the door. All she could think about was a hot bath and twenty-four hours of sleep.

After all her hard, tireless work the members of the committee were finally in place. The first draft of the Women and Minority Action Commission's mission and goals statement was making its rounds. She finally felt as if it was all worthwhile.

Dominique had called earlier to let her know that Max was not going to do jail time but was put into treatment. She was satisfied with that as long as he got the help that he needed and didn't pose a threat to any other woman.

Overall, things were beginning to come together. Everything except her and Spence's relationship. It seemed as if with each passing day they grew further apart, and short of returning to Baton Rouge and giving up all that she'd worked for, she didn't know what else to do. Patrice said to give it time, that this was an adjustment period for both of them and as long as they continued to love each other and be open and honest, things would work out.

She stepped out of her heels and she swore her feet sighed with pleasure. She walked down the short hallway to her bedroom just as her intercom buzzed. She retraced her steps and pressed Talk.

"Yes, who is it?"

"Spence."

For a moment she couldn't process what he'd just said. It didn't make sense. The buzzer sounded again.

This time she released the door, then walked around in a bewildered circle.

Spence? What was he doing here? Oh, my God, he'd come to call it off, tell her face-to-face that it wasn't working. She should have known this was coming, but she wasn't prepared. *Oh, no, please…*

The front doorbell buzzed and her insides leaped. She tried to clear her head while she walked to the door. She would be strong. She wouldn't break down.

Tugging in a breath of resolve, she opened the door. The instant she saw him, whatever resolve she had to let him go dissipated and was replaced with a longing that rocked her to her core.

"Hey, baby," he whispered and swept her into his arms. His kiss was long and slow and sweet, making up for lost time, for all the days and nights he'd been without her. He wanted to consume her, take her essence and meld it with his own so that he would never feel as if he was without her.

A door closing at the end of the hallway drew them reluctantly apart.

Desiree's eyes glowed. She ran her hand over his face as if she couldn't believe that he was real. "What are you doing here?" She took his hand to pull him inside and that was when she noticed the rolling suitcase at his feet.

"That's what I came to talk about."

She stepped aside to let him in and locked the door behind him. The instant the door was locked, he took her to his body again, unable to get his fill of her. He wanted to rememorize every dip, every curve, every inch of her butter-soft flesh.

"I want you," he groaned against her neck, then whispered heated words of love in her ear while he unzipped her skirt, unbuttoned her blouse and relieved her of her bra and panties. Her clothes were in a pool at her feet. He took a moment to step back and look at her and felt as if he was going to explode any minute. "Where's the bedroom?" He reached out and caressed her breast.

Her voice shook. "Down…the hall."

Before she realized what was happening, he picked her up and carried her down the hall. He pushed open the door with his shoulder, crossed the room in three long strides and gently put her down in the center of the bed.

The raw passion in his eyes and the rugged need in his voice were frighteningly intoxicating. He was barely in control and that total sense of abandon fueled her.

She tugged his shirt over his head, stripped the belt from his slacks and pushed his slacks down as far as she could to reach what she sought.

Pleasure engulfed her when she took him into her hand and his entire body shuddered. She understood her power. What it did to him and what it did for her. She felt invincible when she massaged him until he commanded that she stop, that he couldn't take it anymore. It was the way she felt when she was behind the wheel of the Ferrari, all the power was in her total control.

And then he played and teased and taunted and stimulated her until she wept.

When he entered her, pushed himself fully inside of her waiting walls and they declared their love for each other, she knew what heaven on earth really was.

Breathless, damp and satiated, Desiree got as close to Spence as she could, wishing that she could get under his skin.

Hypnotically he stroked her hair, listened to the rhythm of her heart until it had slowed to a normal pace.

"I made a decision," he said softly. He felt her stiffen and continued his soothing stroking. "I've been saying for years that I was going to upgrade Bottoms Up."

Her heart thumped.

"I figured that now was the time."

She rose up on her elbow and looked into his eyes. "What are you saying?"

"I'm saying that a town like D.C. could always use a new jazz restaurant, so why not Bottoms Up II?"

Desiree sprang right up. "You're going to open a new club—here? You're going to move to D.C.?" She gripped his shoulders as if she was ready to shake the answers out of him.

He chuckled from deep in his throat. "Yes and yes. I brought a few things with me, so I hope you can find some room for me until we find a bigger place."

She squealed with delight and covered his face with kisses. Then, just as quickly, she jerked back. "What about the club in Baton Rouge? How are you going to manage both places?"

"My staff is trained very well, which they keep reminding me. It'll be fine. I figure if Emeril can do it, so can I. I've already started checking into some possible locations."

She gave him a playful sock in the arm and stood up. "You didn't say a word to me."

"I didn't want to disappoint you if it didn't work out."

She flopped down on the bed and stared up at the ceiling. Joy filled every inch of her being. Spence would be right there with her. They would cheer each other on. Be there when things got tough. Wake each other in the morning and put each other to sleep at night.

"Desi?"

"Hmm?" She wiggled closer.

"Did I ever tell you how turned on I get seeing you in your racing gear and flying at lightning speeds around the track?"

She grinned and slinked on top of him. She ran her finger across his bottom lip. "No… Why don't you tell me all about it?" she purred as she revved his engine, put him in gear and rode off into their future, which she knew was a road of endless possibilities.

* * * * *